Honor of a Lady

** THE DUELING SEASON IS A
SEQUENTIAL SERIES MEANT TO BE READ
IN ORDER OF PUBLICATION. **

also by shirley marks

REGENCY ROMANCE SERIES

The Dueling Season
Meant to be read in order of publication

Book 1: Honor of a Lady
Book 2: No Higher Opinion
Book 3: Matter of Affection

The Gentlemen of Worth series

The Suitor List
Perfectly Flawed
A Grand Deception
The Duke Dilemma
An Elaborate Hoax
A Rogue Reformed

REGENCY ROMANCE

Miss Quinn's Quandary
An Agreeable Arrangement
His Lordship's Chaperone
** Lady Eugenia's Holiday **

Author's Note

Lady Frances Abbott first appeared in
her sister's book *Lady Eugenia's Holiday*.
Matter of Affection is the conclusion of
her tale.
S.M.

THE DUELING SEASON
BOOK 1

SHIRLEY MARKS

** THE DUELING SEASON IS A
SEQUENTIAL SERIES MEANT TO BE READ
IN ORDER OF PUBLICATION. **

ISBN-13: 978-1-946314-06-2 (PAPERBACK)

ISBN-10: 1-946314-06-4

ISBN-13: 978-1-946314-07-9 (EBOOK)

ISBN-10: 1-946314-07-2

Photographs provided by Unsplashed.com

Jacques Bopp - background

Public Domain:

John Trumbull - Sally Minot portrait

www.ShirleyMarks.com

dedicated to the following ...
in chronological order

Heidi Ashworth (1996)
thank you for writing Ancilla's Story

C Lo (2006)
a family friend who inspired a hero and started
it all

Grace S (2013)
a most charming lady of my acquaintance

Dr E Robinson (2014)
who selected the status and surname of a
heroine

P Walsh (2015)
your wit and cheek,
Drayton Court Hotel, Ealing, London

Mary Beth C (2015)
we will always have Paris

Denise S (2015)
who allowed me to graft from her family tree

Nurse Hefflefinger (2016)
for her kindness and care

and finally...

Rachel and Kim for their comments,
suggestions, and time

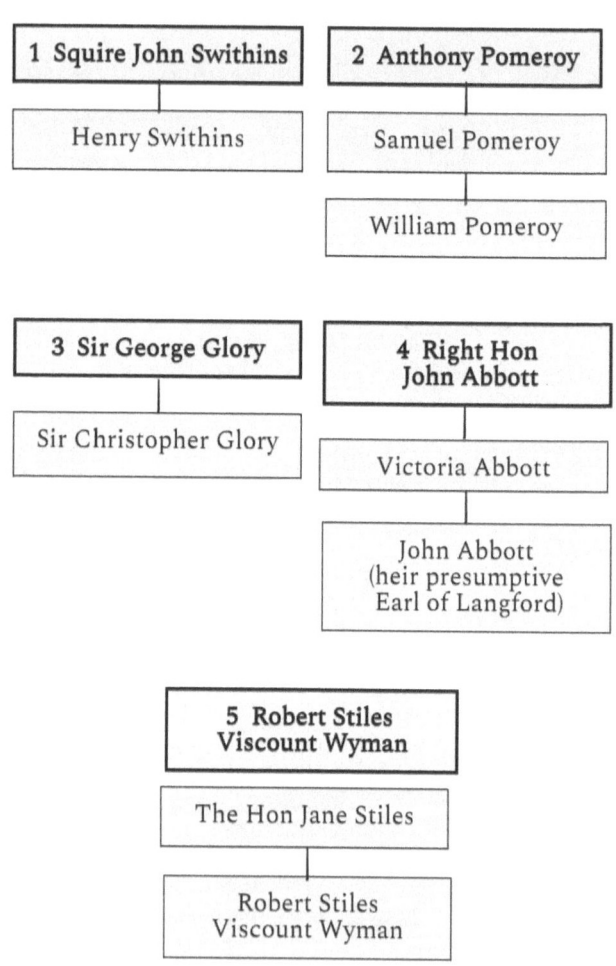

**Grace, Lady Yardley
Early Marriages**

1 Squire John Swithins

Henry Swithins

2 Anthony Pomeroy

Samuel Pomeroy

William Pomeroy

3 Sir George Glory

Sir Christopher Glory

**4 Right Hon
John Abbott**

Victoria Abbott

John Abbott
(heir presumptive
Earl of Langford)

**5 Robert Stiles
Viscount Wyman**

The Hon Jane Stiles

Robert Stiles
Viscount Wyman

Honor of a Lady

** THE DUELING SEASON IS A
SEQUENTIAL SERIES MEANT TO BE READ
IN ORDER OF PUBLICATION. **

one

"Seven! Eight! Nine! Ten!"

The morning was cool and wet, the visibility fair. The mist had only just cleared from the ground minutes before. Both men turned to face one another. They straightened their arms leveling their pistols toward their opponent, taking aim. Sir Christopher Glory stood calmly across from Lord Linwood.

Martin Chandler waited next to the coach with the surgeon, well off the dueling field in what was deemed the *safe area*.

The two men were well-matched marksmen. Christopher was a tolerable shot. Certainly no better than Lord Linwood but neither could have outperformed Martin.

This was exactly why he had not wished to be a second to his friend Kit, he wanted to be the one facing Linwood.

Martin felt his insides seething with pure loathing. It was *his* fiancée whose character had been slandered. Victoria was to be *his* wife in a month's time and now he doubted.... His jaw ached from clenching his teeth, containing his fury.

1

The filthy, lying wretch deserved to die, and Christopher had every right to kill him. Did Linwood feel even an ounce of regret for his actions?

Idiot! Kit had removed his hat and faced him straight on, providing an enormous target. Even Linwood might successfully wound, if not kill, Martin's friend. Christopher had only to turn his shoulder toward his opponent to prove a more difficult target. Instead of covering the front of his shirt with his coat lapels, they lay flat. The white cravat stood out as if it were marking the very spot where Linwood's ball should land.

It would be pure luck if he managed to hit any mark from the twenty pace distance. The pistol in his lordship's hand visibly shook. It gave Martin a great deal of satisfaction to see Linwood's pitiful condition.

By God! Martin could feel himself shaking with rage. Linwood had said horrendous things about his Victoria and *Martin* was the one who wanted satisfaction. If Kit did not pull the trigger soon, Martin would lose all composure and run onto the field and strangle *his lordship* with his bare hands!

Shoot him now!

"Hush, sir," Mr. Braithwaite, the surgeon, whispered. Martin had no idea he had spoken out loud. "We would not wish to disturb the gentlemen's concentration."

Linwood fired first, his pistol emitting a booming sound and a cloud of smoke engulfed the two men. It took a few minutes before it drifted slowly off the center of the field and dissipated. He missed, just as Martin predicted.

Christopher, who had not yet fired, stood in the same spot with his arm, pistol in hand, still by his side.

"Go ahead, Glory," Linwood called out. "Kill me, you've got the right. But it'd be murder."

"That is correct, sir. I do have every right." Christopher called out, clear and strong. "You have cast dishonor onto my family by insulting my sister."

Martin could see the beads of sweat on Linwood's brow. If his lordship ran he'd be branded a coward and never be able to show his face in Town again. The empty pistol slipped from his hand and fell on the ground at his feet.

Kit paused and with a slight lift of his chin he pointed his loaded weapon at his opponent. A pivot, slightly to the left, moving his arm off his target.

He's going to fire wide and miss!

The second gunshot sounded. As the smoke cleared it was soon evident that Sir Christopher had missed. Lord Linwood remained, quaking.

"There you go, Glory, we're done, I say," Linwood shouted. His voice trembled as much as his hand had.

"And so we are." Christopher returned, an easy smile graced his lips. He walked toward Linwood and leaned forward to speak words meant for only his opponent's ears.

Linwood nodded and moved back before stepping away. He gave Christopher a last glance over his shoulder before gathering his retinue and departing.

Christopher retrieved Linwood's fallen weapon then headed for his coach. He handed the pistols to a footman who held the empty velvet-lined box and with a nod to Mr. Braithwaite said, "There is no need for your services today, sir." He inclined his head. "I thank you for coming."

"Thank goodness for that." The surgeon touched the brim of his hat before taking his leave. "I bid good day to you both, then."

"I have gained satisfaction, dear friend," Christopher murmured to Martin while working one glove off.

"But Linwood walks away. How can you allow that?" Martin

ground out, barely able to keep his temper in check. "He said all those wretched things about Victoria and.... How can you tolerate knowing.... She's your sister, man. Don't it matter what he's said about her?" He would not be able to tolerate a slur to his own dear Pauline under the same circumstances. "You have a chance to silence him or wing him, teach him a lesson. But that's not what you did." Martin shook his head. He could not believe what he'd just seen. It was an opportunity lost.

"I fought this duel on your behalf, not Victoria's." Christopher pulled off his remaining glove. "You surely would have killed Linwood, there is no doubt, and then where would you be? Charged with murder? Fleeing the country? And what of Pauline? Who would be her protector?" He handed his footman the soiled gloves he'd shed and pulled out another pair from his coat pocket. Now standing a mere foot away, he met Martin's gaze. "Linwood has said nothing that isn't common knowledge, he don't deserve to die."

"*Common knowledge?*" Martin repeated, taken completely by surprise. What did Kit mean by that? Certainly the accusations of her infidelity, her 'freely bestowing her favors' as Linwood put it, could not be true. If it were so, she was not the female Martin believed her to be.

He loved her...he *thought* he loved her. At this moment, he wasn't quite certain what his feelings were. Anger? Hatred? Betrayal? He certainly did not suffer from a broken heart.

"Vic has behaved abominably. If you had faced Linwood in your current state you would have had no trouble dropping him to the ground, I have no doubt. I am not about to risk your or my life to preserve what honor Vic may have left, if any. Now that the duel is over" —Christopher drew on a new glove and stepped around his friend— "You need to ask yourself what are *you* going to do about it? Is Victoria truly the type of woman you want to marry?"

The importance of the matter came to him. If what Linwood alleged, and Kit now confirmed was true, then simply taking aim and pulling a trigger would not solve Martin's problem. That would have been too easy a solution.

Martin looked away from Kit to the surrounding trees, noting the growing light illuminating the branches and leaves. Now that Linwood's insult had been settled Martin needed to extricate himself from Victoria. Their marriage could not take place. How would that come about? That might require a skill he did not possess.

THE FOUR WOMEN IN THE FRONT PARLOR OF GRAYSON HOUSE DID not wait calmly. They had been awake far earlier than any of them were used to rising, dressed long before they were used to dressing, and they now sat or stood, or paced, without having their usual breakfast.

The news had arrived from outside of this house. Lady Yardley's maid had it from her friend who was told by her brother last night. He had been informed by a friend of Lord Ortone's younger brother's valet who had heard the news from his friend, name unknown, who overheard it from one of Lord Linwood's seconds relaying the incident that led up to the instigation of the duel at White's Gentlemen's Club the previous evening before the start of the Partridge rout.

That was how the females residing at Grayson House knew to rise early and wait belowstairs, hopefully for Christopher's safe return and to learn the outcome of the not-so-secret affair.

All were too nervous to sit down to breakfast and took turns pacing the carpeted parlor floor.

"All will be well, Mama. Shall I pour you a bit more tea?" Jane Stiles sat next to her mother, Grace, Lady Yardley, and tried her best to comfort her parent.

"Yes, thank you, dear. I fear it must be growing cold." Far from being an elderly woman, Lady Yardley lifted the cup and saucer she held with both hands as if she were far older than her six and thirty years.

"That's all right, Miss Jane, allow me." Mrs. Heffelfinger, Jane's aunt and chaperone, intervened and moved to retrieve the pot from the tray. "We've yet to put up your hair this morning."

"My hair, Auntie?" Jane glared at Mrs. Heffelfinger incredulously. "What care I of my *hair* when my brother faces such peril?"

"*Peril?*" Mrs. Heffelfinger all but scoffed. "I don't think it will be as bad as that, do you, Lady Yardley?"

"I cannot imagine Christopher to be so careless as to allow himself to be shot. I confess...I have many sons and if I were to make my secret known, although perhaps I should not, that he is my favorite among them. He is all too kind to intercede as the head of the family when Harry really should do his duty as the eldest."

"But Harry is far too busy managing his father's estates," Jane defended her eldest half-brother's absence.

"Squire Swithins," Lady Yardley uttered the name of her beloved first husband on a sigh. "God rest his soul."

"Then there are both the Pomeroy brothers, Samuel and William, who might have stepped in but must needs continue their father's business," Jane continued. She knew the members of her immediate family well but it never hurt to recite them, especially when she had the time.

"My dear second husband Anthony. God rest his soul." Lady Yardley's eyes misted at his memory. "However, Christopher takes care of us all, and he is but one and twenty himself. I know that his father, my dear third husband Sir George, God rest his soul, would have been so very proud."

"I do wish I could claim to be a stronger relation," Mrs. Heffelfinger turned away from the group and sighed, continuing with more than a touch of concern in her voice. "Since my dear Jane is only his half-sister, and I, her aunt, my connection to him is tenuous, to be sure. I completely agree that Sir Christopher truly deserves your kind words, ma'am. I do hope he comes out of this in fine form."

"I knew he would be in danger!" Jane turned to address her older sister. "I do not know how you can sit there and remain calm when *all this* is happening because of *you*."

"Because of *me*?" Rising from the overstuffed chair, Lady Yardley's eldest daughter Victoria crossed to the hearth. "I can hardly understand why you would blame all this on me. *I* wasn't even in attendance when the disagreement occurred."

"Although we do not know *why*," Jane's tone turned quiet. "We do know it has something to do regarding you, Vic."

"And don't you think it is rather *romantic* that two gentlemen are dueling over me?" Victoria posed the question sounding quite detached from the entire matter. Had she risen with the rest of them because she was worried for Kit or because she was curious of the outcome?

"Not when one of the participants is your brother." Mrs. Heffelfinger interrupted. "I have my own thoughts on what *that* means and if I were to venture on the reasons for the duel they would not put you in a flattering light, Miss Victoria."

After the companion's pointed remarks directed to Victoria,

she swept her gaze around the room pausing on Lady Yardley and then Jane, giving each a knowing nod of her head.

The women had been awake for hours, waiting for Christopher's return. *If* he were to return…of course he would return. Jane would not accept any other outcome.

Their tea had been replaced with several fresh pots. Each person had taken several turns about the room, singularly or in pairs to pass the time. The longer the minutes, hours passed with no word of the duel's outcome, the thicker the tension grew in the room.

Then male voices were heard, just outside in the corridor or from the foyer. *He* had returned, for it must have been he. The women turned toward the doors and froze, waiting to see who had arrived and to hear the news they had brought.

CHRISTOPHER, ACCOMPANIED BY MARTIN CHANDLER, ENTERED through the double doors of the front parlor and drew the full attention of the four ladies within.

"Kit!" Jane ran into her brother's arms, tears of relief had been shed and now streaked down her face at his entrance. "Thank goodness you are all right! We were afraid you might have been killed!"

"Killed?" Christopher replied somewhat taken aback. "Nonsense."

There was no need for Lady Yardley to stand, her son came to her with his youngest sister held tight by his side.

"No *cry of relief* that I have returned unharmed, my dear?" Martin leveled this less than lover-like remark at his fiancée.

"You did not face Lord Linwood on the field, Martin," she replied. "There is no reason that you should have been harmed."

"But I was your brother's Second and you do not know what may have transpired. What if I needed to intervene or step-in? You cannot have known."

"Alas, you both are here, clearly unharmed." Victoria took his hand in both of hers. "I am glad to see you well."

Martin pulled his hand from Victoria, not pleased at all.

"Well, Christopher, what happened? What were you fighting about?" Lady Yardley near-begged her son but did not allow him time to speak. "Dreadful business, this dueling. How were we to know the outcome? You leave the females to wring their hands while you gentlemen wander off without a thought to our nerves."

"It is not done to vex you, dear ma'am, I can assure you." Christopher set Jane upon her feet, determining she felt quite the thing again. His sister's tears were gone and she made one last sniff.

"Really? I daresay some word from you, of what happened out there would have—"

"He deloped! That's what happened." Martin answered impatiently in a stern voice, almost a shout.

Christopher had listened to his friend's ire during the entire journey home. Apparently that was not enough time to come to terms with the outcome.

"You should have killed him, Kit." Martin still sounded angry.

"Oh, no. Linwood's a cur, not a liar. And a remarkably bad shot at that. Did you see the way his hand was shaking? Poor fellow."

"*Poor fellow?* How can you possibly say that after...after...." Martin silenced once he noted his friend's frown. No, it was not a topic that should be discussed in this company.

"Now that we have established that I am quite well, may we

get on with our lives?" Christopher glanced about the room. "I would like to rid myself of the travel dirt and change my clothes before sitting down to some breakfast. However, before I can do either, I must speak to you, ma'am" —he inclined his head toward his mother— "and to you, Vic."

"Am I to leave?" Jane remarked, sounding quite offended.

"What I have to say does not concern you, my dear."

"Come now, Miss Jane, let me take you abovestairs and we'll fix your hair." Mrs. Heffelfinger tried her best to distract her niece.

"Enough about my *hair*, Aunt," she exclaimed in exasperation.

"If you please, Jane." Christopher entreated with exaggerated patience that she so disliked.

"Oh! The pair of you!" Jane turned to her mother for a reprieve. "Mama?"

"I'm sure you will learn what transpires soon enough. Now do as your brother bids."

"Very well." Jane was not at all pleased and turned to Mrs. Heffelfinger. "Shall we go then, Auntie?" The two ladies linked arms. The younger one tilted her chin a bit higher to demonstrate her displeasure before quitting the parlor.

Silence suffused the room. The occupants turned to Christopher and he took his time to address them.

"There is no need for me to stay, I am sure. Shall I bid you all a good day?" Martin, who clearly battled with the blue devils since the fateful night of the disagreement regarding Victoria's virtue, felt he had no cause to remain, even with his fiancée present.

"I believe this will be of interest to you, Martin. I beg that you remain."

"If you insist." Martin's deep intake of air and the length of time he held it, displayed his patience.

Christopher gestured to the doors. "Will you be so good as to provide us with some privacy?"

Martin's near-silent grumbling, a sound to which Christopher was acutely attuned, had nothing to do with the task but with his request to stay. Martin closed the parlor doors and sat in an armchair next to him, as far as possible from his intended.

It was clear *theirs* was not a loving couple's reunion. Victoria did not regard Martin's presence with any particular kindness, and Martin did not gaze upon his fiancée with particular affection.

"Vic, I have done my duty and stood up for your honor as a brother should, however, I am unwilling to place blame entirely on Lord Linwood when all he did was tell the truth."

"What was it he said that caused offense?" Lady Yardley turned to her son.

Christopher inhaled, taking a moment to rephrase the original insult for feminine ears. "It ran somewhere along the lines of...it was a shame Martin had taken the bother to marry her when her wares were freely given."

Lady Yardley gasped. "He did not! Say it is not so!" She brought her hand to her mouth which did little to conceal the rising color in her face.

Victoria gazed heavenward. Christopher felt it was not the reaction of an innocent.

Martin cleared his throat, seeming discomfort at his presence in this family matter.

"I am afraid so," Christopher admitted. "Of course, ma'am, it was Martin who is the true injured party here, not Vic. It may be a game for you, *ma soeur,* you have greatly wronged my friend, but he was quite attached—as you should have been."

Lady Yardley, still overcome by the nature of Victoria's insult, could not speak.

"Kit, you are too horrible for words." Victoria did not show the least bit of discomfort at the accusation.

"I would not say such a thing if it were not true, sister." Christopher would not allow her to escape this incident without making amends. "Now that the duel has been fought, I expect what is left of your honor has been maintained. Whether you have any remnant of such, I cannot say."

"Christopher!" his mother cried.

"If you have any sense of decency, ma'am." Martin rounded on Victoria in a very hard and sudden manner, clearly doing his utmost to maintain control. "I beg you give me my *congé.*"

"It would save *your* reputation, would it not?" Victoria replied in hauteur.

"I have no concern regarding *my* reputation." He took his time to form each word. "From my understanding, Lord Linwood's allegations appear to be true. I do not wish to cause you further harm but it is clear to me that although your heart, if you have one, may be untouched, mine—" There was a catch in his voice, momentarily silencing him. "I am not so unaffected." He fell silent again, blinked back the moisture in his eyes, and drew in a breath before continuing. "As you can imagine this dreadful incident finishes our engagement."

"Oh, do not say so," Lady Yardley managed. "Our families have grown very close, indeed, these past few months. Why there is you and Christopher. And just look at Jane and your little Pauline, they are the best of friends. Would you see that come to an end?"

"No, ma'am, I would not," Martin admitted. "And I see no reason it should be so."

"The *associations* between the two families may remain.

However—" Christopher remarked but a sterner tone told of the approaching seriousness of their situation. "Because of the unseemly gossip I expect to arise from the duel, as it does in such cases, I have made arrangements for you, my lady, to accompany Victoria to Bath for the remainder of the Season. Lady Belton is expecting us. We leave this afternoon."

"Bath!" Victoria shrieked. "No one, who is anyone, goes to Bath anymore!"

"You may feel right at home there, I daresay. You have been the cause of this Scandal and it is only right you pay the consequences, not Martin who should be free to remain in Town."

"I believe it is a reasonable resolution," Martin replied. "There is no chance that we will accidentally come across one another."

Christopher had already decided upon Victoria's relocation, convinced that it was the best for all concerned. Life, as he imagined, would have a very good chance of returning to normal.

"I have written to Lady Belton, accepting her hospitality on your behalf."

"It will be good to see Tilly," Lady Yardley commented. "It has been an age. How good of her to invite us."

"I expect you will not find Bath lacking in amusement, Vic." Christopher hoped Victoria would do her utmost to find a husband there. It would be impossible, after this morning's incident, for both to remain in Town. "There is Society."

"*Old* Society!" was his sister's comment. "It is inhabited by old men, widows, and broken down sailors!"

"Mama should find her next husband if she is of a mind to do so," Christopher replied, trying to sound encouraging.

"Do not say such things." Lady Yardley fanned her warming face to cool herself. The color swept up her neck reaching her cheeks. "I am an old woman, far too old to think of marriage again." She paused as if pondering the idea of another husband before fully rejecting it. "Oh, no!"

"I do beg you, ma'am, that you do not settle for anyone below the rank of duke else you will be doing yourself a great disservice on your ascent of the Social ladder."

"Oh, Christopher, you are too monstrous to say so!" his parent scolded him.

"All your many years, your hard work will be for naught." He shook his head and delighted in teasing her.

"No. No—you abominable boy!" She rose from her chair and crossed to the double doors to exit. "I am off to pack now."

"I must admit that she is quite charming," Christopher commented with a smile. "I can see how any gentleman would find her enchanting. There is not an unpleasant bone in her body. You have inherited much from her, Vic."

"Careful, Kit. That comes dangerously close to resembling a compliment." Victoria tried to take the position of the victim—a younger sister being abused by her elder brother...which, as far as Christopher was concerned, was far from the truth. "Martin may get the idea you've changed your mind and insist our engagement should stand."

"No such thing, my girl. It's a shame you cannot learn more from our parent." Christopher imagined the inspiration Lady Yardley elicited in a suitor. "She has the power to unwillingly captivate men and they fall willingly at her feet and forfeit what they must to make her their own—for they understand she has become the center of their world. You, my dear sister, should be more discerning regarding your choice of gentleman."

"You are hateful, brother," Victoria responded in a violent hiss. "Hateful!" She pushed past him to quit the room and he caught her upper arm to stay her until he had finished.

"It is of no matter. You may or may not choose to make

preparations for the journey but I will personally see to it that you are seated in that coach when we leave." Christopher sounded as insistent and sage as any older brother. "The welfare of our many younger brothers may not be of concern to you but I must see to their well-being, consider their futures, as well as Jane's, until they come of age."

"Will you kindly unhand me?" Victoria appeared not to care what he said. She glared at Martin as if he had something to do with deciding her unpleasant fate. "I hope *you* are satisfied."

"I am happy to say, ma'am, that we are at an end. I have nothing more to say to you." Martin displayed a polite, tight smile. "I bid you a good day. Kit," he acknowledged his friend with the nod of his head before leaving.

"It would be for the good of both our families," Christopher continued to his sister, "if you would quietly withdraw from the notice of Society and allow this disgrace to pass. The outcome may be minor and all forgotten in the space of a month or two, certainly by Season's end." He released his hold on her arm and, without a further word, Victoria stalked out of the room.

For Christopher, partaking in a duel, planning an expeditious journey, and alienating a sibling all before sitting down to breakfast was quite enough for one morning.

ENTERING THE CONDUIT STREET HOUSE, MARTIN HANDED HIS hat, coat, and gloves to the footman and planned to head straight for his bed. Even though he had skipped breakfast, he had no appetite now. His morning was an emotional drain filled with frustration, disappointment, and anger.

He started toward the staircase when he heard his mother call out.

"Martin? Is that you?"

"Yes, ma'am." He could not keep the forced indulgent tone from permeating his reply to his parent. Stopping at the base of the staircase, Martin closed his eyes, curbing his need for immediate solitude, took a deep breath, and headed down the corridor toward the breakfast room.

"Heavens!" Mrs. Chandler straightened in her chair, looked up from her plate of buttered eggs, and set her steaming cup of coffee onto its saucer. "Are you just coming home now? At this hour?"

Martin took a moment to appreciate the scene before him. Lingering over a simple cup of coffee, contemplating a hearty breakfast while perusing the morning paper, perhaps? Enjoying the company of one's family—even at this difficult moment. This was domesticity that might be out of his reach.

"No, Mama." Pauline studied him carefully, taking in his clothing…his jacket…his boots. "As you see he is not in evening dress. He's been out already this morning—though he's not been riding."

His sister was too keen an observer to keep much from her. Martin met her gaze hoping she could not read his thoughts. She could not have an inkling of what he had been doing. If she had known, she would have bombarded him with questions when he had first entered.

"Where have you been?" Mrs. Chandler eyed her son from toe to head. "Your boots are filthy."

"Yes, ma'am. I've been *out*." And that was all he was prepared to divulge about his whereabouts. He did not wish to discuss his early morning activities at present. Martin's cravat felt tight around his neck and he found it difficult to wait to shed his jacket. Perhaps later, later today or tomorrow, he would bring up the topic of Kit's duel, although he expected they would hear *talk* of what had occurred before then.

"Out? Where can you have gone?" His mother placed her palms on the table before her, taking a sterner attitude. "*Before* this hour, for you are presently home and presumably finished with whatever-it-was that had occupied you."

"Suffice it to say, ma'am, all that is important for you to know is that as of today, my engagement to Miss Victoria Abbott has come to an end."

"You have not returned from an elopement, have you?" Mrs. Chandler's eyes widened and she pressed her hand to her throat.

"No, Mama." Pauline quickly laid her hand over her mother's to divert her attention from her brother. "Martin has done nothing of the sort, I can assure you. He would never do anything so reprehensible."

"Your father would be outraged! He's been looking forward to attending the wedding since Christmas!"

Martin doubted his father cared where the nuptials took place as long as the deed was done. That was why he remained at their country house and arranged for his arrival only a few days before the wedding ceremony.

"She's handed *you* the mitten, then?" Mrs. Chandler continued to search for the dissolution of his engagement.

Martin merely answered, "We agreed that we would not suit."

"What do you mean by *not suit*? After all this time?"

"That is very sad to hear, Martin." Pauline's downcast demeanor portrayed a sorrow he could not feel himself. "I think it is much better you learn now than make the mistake of marrying her."

"Agreed." Martin bowed. "If you will excuse me, I believe I need to retire to my room." It was not yet noon and yet the day had already felt extraordinarily long.

"Of course, Martin." The sympathetic intonation came from his sister. "Martin?"

He turned back to face his family.

"Is there anything we can do for you?" Her small, compassionate voice was very comforting. There was no doubt that his sister cared.

"No, thank you, *pet*. I believe right now I'd like to rest." He smiled at his sister and walked from the breakfast room to ascend the staircase.

His life, he felt at this very moment, was a complete shambles, an utter ruin, through no fault of his own. It could have been far worse if Kit had not intervened and persuaded Victoria to break their engagement. It was so very clear now that she was not a good choice for a wife.

He should have felt shattered that the woman he loved had betrayed him.

He *would* have felt shattered if he had truly *loved* her. Perhaps that was the crux of the matter. He really had not loved her, although he had done his utmost, over these last six months, to convince himself that he had.

It was not the upset of his pending marriage that made him feel blue-deviled. It was that he had not loved her. He hadn't truly felt angry at Victoria, the faithless female who had betrayed him. He felt angry that his plans for his future had been ruined.

At this moment he wished only to be alone. Perhaps, he thought, he was not the marriage-minded type. Perhaps he was the kind of man who needed a lifetime of solitude. There would be time for that in years to come. Once he took up his own residence and Pauline had married and moved away to start her own family.

With no wife, no children of his own, Martin imagined that life would be sad for him, indeed.

two

"I AM SO VERY sad to see them leave." Now properly coiffed, Jane stood at the window facing the street and watched their family's traveling coaches pass before the townhouse on their departure. "I will miss them a great deal."

"Come away from there, my dear." Mrs. Heffelfinger waved Jane away from the window. "It can do no good to pine after them. Never worry, your brother shall return soon enough and you will have his company once more."

"I know but still...." Jane sighed. She was very close to her family and to remain in Town without them, even for a little while, was too sad to contemplate. "I know Vic has been naughty but to send her away is a horrid thing."

"We don't know what she's done. I expect Sir Christopher would not have set such a harsh penance if her conduct had not warranted such. And I must say that Bath, my dear, is hardly a punishment." Mrs. Heffelfinger led her niece from the window to the sofa and chairs where they seated themselves. "From what I could glean, I expect her ill-deeds are much worse than we can imagine and— Though I can only speak for myself, I honestly believe I do not wish to know."

Jane sighed again and made a moue.

"Perhaps we should find some way to keep ourselves occupied until your brother's return. I believe there is some mending to be done or, if you would like, you may start a new embroidery pattern." Mrs. Heffelfinger tried her best to sound encouraging but the reality of what lie ahead could not be kept hidden. "There'll be no parties or gatherings for us for the next week without Sir Christopher's escort."

"I expect not." Jane was not *Out* yet and her social life only included a small group of friends and parties given by family acquaintances. Even those activities would be curtailed without her brother's presence.

"What I fear is there will be news of the duel whispered about Town and we need not fan those flames. We can only hope that talk of this morning's incident is forgotten before he returns and we can go about without any hint of scandal."

"I suppose so." Jane accepted her aunt's word on the matter without truly understanding the whole of her meaning. "Perhaps this afternoon I will write to Victoria."

"I'm sure she will be glad to hear from you. A kind word from your quarter must always be welcome." Mrs. Heffelfinger assured her charge. "Yes, that is a very good idea."

"Perhaps she will write back and tell me what she's done to warrant this horrible treatment from Kit." Jane could always hope. But it was not her sister's way to confide in anyone, especially when she'd been naughty.

"I believe it best we keep in the shadows for this, to be sure," Mrs. Heffelfinger suggested.

"You may not wish to know, ma'am, but I, for one, cannot

help but feel curious." Jane could not even imagine what her sister could have done for so harsh a punishment.

"I don't know what Sir Christopher will say about her taking you into her confidence." Mrs. Heffelfinger shook her head, changing her mind. "Yes, I do. He will say you are too young."

"Oh, *pooh!*" Jane stood at the indignation of, once again, 'being too young.' She really was tired of hearing that. "Sometimes Kit can be so—"

"I beg your pardon, ladies." Both ladies turned to stare at Liddell when he appeared, quite soundlessly, at the door. "Mrs. Chandler and Miss Chandler have arrived."

"Well, Liddell, see them in at once." Mrs. Heffelfinger motioned for Jane to come stand next to her and wait for their guests.

Soon Mrs. Chandler and Pauline appeared. They had not removed their outer garments.

"Good day to you, Miss Stiles, Mrs. Heffelfinger," Mrs. Chandler greeted.

An odd tension filled the air. It seemed unusual since the four of them had previously rubbed along well, especially Jane and Pauline. They were, had been, the best of friends. What had happened to cause this very awkward formal address?

"And to you, Mrs. Chandler, Miss Chandler," Mrs. Heffelfinger replied. "I hope you both are doing well. Will you not come in and be seated? Allow me to call for some tea."

"I do not believe we will be remaining for any significant period of time," Mrs. Chandler's clipped tone revealed her unease. "We had hoped to speak to Sir Christopher but it seems we have come too late."

"Kit has gone to Bath," Jane informed them. "He is escorting Mama and Victoria. I believe he expects to return by the end of the week."

"To Bath?" Mrs. Chandler seemed taken aback by the news.

"May we be of assistance, Mrs. Chandler?" Mrs. Heffelfinger had every good intention of helping but, in fact, knew nothing more than the person posing the questions.

"We will surely tell Kit you wish to speak to him when he returns," Jane offered.

"I was hoping to learn...."

"Surely Mr. Chandler has informed you of this morning's—" Mrs. Heffelfinger began.

"No, he has not, and that is the most vexsome part."

"Martin has said nothing of.... *Something* is amiss," Pauline interrupted her mother. "In fact, he has said *nothing* at all."

She paused to compose herself. Jane would have understood but her mother would have been horrified to see a public outburst as if the present company had not consisted of her dearest friends.

"As we understand, *Miss Abbott* has handed him the mitten."

Their once very close family friend Mrs. Chandler referred to Victoria as *Miss Abbott*?

"We were lucky to learn that much. We have no idea how this has come about." Mrs. Chandler voiced her concerns without the benefit of Sir Christopher's presence. "We were hoping he could shed some light on what has happened between the two."

"Do you know?" Pauline stared wide-eyed at her friend who remained uncharacteristically quiet. Oh, if only she and Jane could be private! Pauline would soon learn everything her friend knew without further hesitation.

"Why do you not sit with us and allow me to ring for a tray," Mrs. Heffelfinger offered again. "I believe we may be able to enlighten you as to a *bit* of what has transpired. You will wish to be seated for this, I can assure you."

"We are all affected by this nasty business. I suppose we must take part in clearing the air as well, however...I had hoped to learn more."

With one look from her mother, Pauline followed her mother's lead and untied the ribbons to her bonnet then unfastened her pelisse for an extended stay. The ladies gathered in the parlor. The four sat close together and leaned with their heads forward while they spoke in hushed tones.

"We had news that Sir Christopher was to fight a duel this morning." Mrs. Heffelfinger whispered in strict confidence.

"A duel!" Mrs. Chandler straightened and gasped. Her eyes grew wide and she leveled a desperate gaze at her daughter. "You don't think that's where Martin—"

THAT WAS DREADFUL! PAULINE REALIZED THAT MUST HAVE BEEN where her brother had gone that morning. She couldn't believe he would leave the house on such business and not say a word.

"Your vinaigrette, Mama?" Pauline placed her hand on her mother's arm in case she would need aid, ready to search her parent's reticule. Mrs. Chandler shook her head, refusing the need for the *sal volatile*.

Pauline knew Sir Christopher must have emerged unharmed for he was at this very moment on his way to Bath with Lady Yardley and Victoria.

"Martin was Kit's second," Jane added.

"Who was the opponent?" Mrs. Chandler found her voice.

"Lord Linwood," Mrs. Heffelfinger replied.

"Linwood...Linwood...." Mrs. Chandler squinted, trying her best to recall if he was known to her. "His name is not familiar to me."

"And all we know is that it had something to do with Victoria," Jane concluded.

"Protecting her *honor* I suppose...." Mrs. Chandler sounded somewhat doubtful. "Why did Martin not take part himself—Thank goodness he did not!" Mrs. Chandler gazed heavenward, presumably in thanks that her son was not bodily involved. "I'm certain it must have something to do with their break, for you must know their betrothal is at an end. I wonder what could have happened?"

"Kit said Martin had no right to face Linwood, he was only her fiancé and not her brother."

"Martin would have killed him." Pauline knew her brother to be a superb marksman. If it were not for Sir Christopher's intervention, Lord Linwood would now be dead.

"Kit said he participated not on Victoria's behalf but Martin's," Jane repeated what she had heard her brother say earlier.

"Mr. Chandler would have had to flee the country if he'd killed Lord Linwood." Mrs. Heffelfinger voiced a concern no other dared to state out loud.

"We have Sir Christopher to thank for that." Mrs. Chandler seemed to be resting a bit easier now that she'd received some satisfactory answers to her questions.

"And now that Martin and Victoria have parted, what of our friendship?" Jane turned toward Pauline. The two young ladies, very near the same age, who had much in common, became fast friends when Jane's half-sister, Victoria, and Pauline's brother decided to marry at the end of last year's Season.

The two families had spent a joyful and festive Christmas at Barlow Hall, Oxfordshire then traveled to Parklands, the Chandler's family country house in neighboring Hertfordshire. They welcomed the new year and the following Twelfth Night celebration together.

"This has been a very sad business. Martin is in an awful state," replied Mrs. Chandler. "What a horrid start to the Season. Simply ghastly. Perhaps we should return to Hertfordshire. I think Martin would welcome such an idea."

"What of your promise to me, Mama?" Pauline knew the primary reason for coming to London was for Martin and Victoria's wedding but she understood they would participate in rounds of parties, balls, and assemblies for her amusement as well. As selfish as it sounded, she had no wish to give up what had been promised to her.

"Thank goodness we have no plans to go out," Mrs. Chandler told her daughter. "I cannot imagine facing anyone who would bring up this morning's incident. I daresay we will be lucky if we can somehow avert a scandal." She turned to Jane and Mrs. Heffelfinger. "Tonight we are to dine at home. I am entertaining a friend and her daughter. Will you not join us, ladies? You would be very welcome, I daresay."

Jane glanced at her aunt who nodded. "Thank you, Mrs. Chandler. It will be very nice to step out of the house after a few days' confinement."

"Then we shall expect you at seven. I will need to inform Cook we have two additional guests." Mrs. Chandler stood slowly, readying to leave. "I wonder if we could coax Martin out of his bedchamber?"

"I doubt it, Mama." Pauline knew the dark, brooding mood which her brother currently wallowed would not be easily vanquished. "I believe he would find a room filled with females a bit intimidating and not at all to his taste."

"*Intimidating?*" Mrs. Chandler swayed a bit. "Don't be ridiculous, dear. Martin does not find females *intimidating* in the least."

LATER THAT DAY, BERNARD, LORD EMERSON, SAT BEHIND HIS DESK in the library and looked forward to the quiet evening that lay before him. His wife, the charming Lady Emerson, was to accompany their son Russell to some society party, leaving his lordship, blissfully alone.

They were to leave not soon enough for his lordship.

The first item on Emerson's agenda was to exchange his cravat, waistcoat, and jacket for the comfort of his banyon, a style of dress his lady would never tolerate. The second item would be to recline in the wingback chair before the hearth with a glass of brandy in one hand and a good book in the other.

Consulting his timepiece, he was anxious for the moment he could relax and find true peace. Even now he could feel the buzz of activity in the air.

Her ladyship's toilette was currently in progress. It took many hours. His son's whereabouts were unknown to him. Russell could be abovestairs at this very moment also preparing for this evening's festivities or he could currently be out and about, waiting until the last moment before rushing home to ready himself for the evening. It was impossible for his lordship to know.

Those two were the social ones of the family, staying up until the early morning hours at balls, soirees, and such. His lordship drew in a breath and would wait patiently over the next few hours for his beloved family members to depart.

A footman approached in silence and presented a silver salver to his lordship, upon it lay a letter. Emerson took up the missive, broke the seal, which he recognized as his solicitor's, and read the contents.

The message informed him of a duel that had occurred at Hampstead Heath that morning between Lord Linwood and Sir Christopher Glory. Apparently, the young baronet had taken exception to the slur spouted by Lord Linwood, who had cast aspersions upon the character of Sir Christopher's sister Miss Victoria Abbott. Both gentlemen survived and there were no injuries.

Miss Victoria Abbott. The earl pondered for a bit. The name sounded familiar. *Abbott...Abbott....*

Good God! Russell's nearly intended was Lady Frances Abbott. There was a family connection. That was the reason for the solicitor's missive. Lady Emerson would not like it.

"My dear." Emerson stood and smiled when his wife entered wearing a deep green evening gown. Her styled hair, piled on her head, sported three white ostrich feathers. He did not exactly hide the note from her but he delayed bringing it to her immediate attention. Once she read its contents...he had the unsettling feeling it would be a very long time until he enjoyed another bout of his treasured peace and quiet.

"How lovely you look, my dear."

"Thank you, my lord." The compliment made her puff up with pride and stand a bit taller. She primped for her husband, showing off a bit. "Have you seen Russell about?"

"No, but never fear, your escort will not fail you." His lordship wondered if she would change her mind about attending a party once she'd read the note. She surely would not be in the mood for an evening of levity.

"Of course you are right." She adjusted her emerald and diamond necklet and stared pointedly at the surface of his desk. "What is that under your hand?"

"Oh...." Emerson glanced at his wife, dreading her response to unpleasant news, and with a great sigh, he folded the note and passed it to her. "I believe you will wish to see this."

Lady Emerson took the correspondence from her husband.

She lowered herself onto the chair beside her and lightly rested her forearms on the table as she began to unfold the note. Emerson wondered exactly how long it would be until my lady fully understood the missive's contents.

"No!" she cried out, pushing onto her feet. "This cannot be."

"Am I correct in my recollection that Sir Christopher Glory is cousin to Russell's Frances?"

Lady Emerson eased onto the chair once again and replied without emotion, "Sir Christopher is half-brother to Miss Victoria Abbott, Lady Frances' cousin. Miss Abbott's brother John is heir presumptive to the Langford earldom. There is no mistaking the family connection."

"I was afraid of that." Emerson began to tap his fingers on the desk.

"I cannot think we would allow our family to marry into theirs. The remotest possibility of scandal must be avoided."

"I was afraid of that as well." His fingers stilled.

Lady Emerson refolded the missive. "I will send my regrets to Lady Bridgeport. We cannot possibly attend her rout this evening." My lady touched the jewels at her throat which must have reminded her of the last few hours spent at the dressing table and gave a sigh of disappointment.

She would not be the only one. For Emerson, there would be no comfortable banyon, glass of brandy, or good book this night.

Lady Emerson stood once again, readying herself to leave and attend to her tasks. "I will also write to Lord and Lady Langford, informing them that Russell and Frances' engagement has ended."

They were sad words to hear for Russell had been elated to have finally made the match after losing Lady Frances during her first Season to Lord Adolphus Barker two years before.

"We are fortunate that we have not gone so far as to make a formal announcement." Lady Emerson stated in thoughtfulness. "No one will know of their arrangement."

"Russell will be disappointed."

"As am I, dear. But we cannot possibly allow it to stand."

"No, I suppose we cannot." Emerson could see his wife's point and understood completely.

Lord and Lady Emerson fell into silence and their son appeared at the door. Sir Russell Crawford detected the uncomfortable atmosphere in his father's library. His mother's normal jubilant demeanor appeared anything but.

Russell had spent an inordinate amount of time preparing for this evening's party. He was happy to do so because he knew his beloved Frances would attend.

"What has happened?" Russell, looking very fine, felt the gloomy mood in the room.

Lady Emerson turned to her son. "Your father and I are trying to prevent our family being embroiled in a scandal."

"What scandal?"

"Suffice it to say your marriage to Lady Frances Abbott cannot go forward."

"What?" Russell replied in a mixture of confusion and anger. "You don't understand, I wish to marry her with all my heart."

"Your father and I will not allow it."

"But our families have already agreed that Fan and I are to wed." Russell's cravat grew tight around his throat, causing him further discomfort.

"*This* family has changed their minds. The Abbotts have

brought scandal to themselves. We have no wish to link our names to theirs."

The world has gone mad.

Russell loved Frances, *loved* her, and he intended to marry her. No matter what his parents—his mother, had decided.

"You are free to go to the theater or out to your club if you wish. We will not be attending the Bridgeport rout tonight," Lady Emerson informed him. "I have no wish to be seen in public."

Russell inclined his head, relaying to his mother he had heard and understood. He did not agree with her, nor did he intend to abide by her wishes.

"I am writing to Lord Langford to formally withdraw your marriage proposal." Her ladyship walked past her son and out of the room.

That very well might be what she would do, Russell thought. *He* would do something altogether different.

three

LADY FRANCES ABBOTT STOOD in the foyer of the South Audley Street house where she resided with her family. She and her mother Lady Langford had only just donned their mantles to leave for a party when a footman arrived to deliver a letter. He wore the blue and yellow Emerson livery and did not wait for a reply. She barely had a chance to contemplate what news could have been so great to warrant sending a message at this hour.

Lord Langford, to whom the letter was addressed, broke the seal, opened, and read the contents. His expression did not exactly alter but he grew a bit paler.

"My dear, I think you will want to see this. I hardly know what to say." His lordship motioned her to the parlor with the wave of his hand. "I believe it may be best if you are seated before you do so."

"Gracious...could it be as bad as all that?" Lady Langford allowed her husband to lead her from the foyer. Frances followed her parents and seated herself on the pink and white striped sofa next to her mother.

"Here you are, my dear." With an artful motion, Lord Langford handed the missive to his wife.

Lady Langford read the letter for herself while Frances looked on. "What is it?" My lady brought her hand to her bejeweled throat and gasped in shock. She furrowed her brows and pursed her lips showing displeasure.

"Will you be all right, my dear?" Lord Emerson kept protectively near, hovering next to her in case she should grow faint. "Shall I fetch the hartshorn? Call for your maid?"

Lady Langford inhaled deeply. "No. No. I shall be fine." She held him at arm's length, but her hand grasped his sleeve for support.

"What does it say, Mama?" Frances glanced at the missive that now rested in her mother's lap but could not quite read it. She had no notion what news could cause her mother's reaction.

"This says...it is impossible for you and Sir Russell to marry. The engagement is at an end."

"But why?" It was happening to her again. Frances now had a second broken engagement. It was dreadful, horrible news. "Does it give a reason?"

"This states that Sir Christopher Glory has participated in a duel this morning with Lord Linwood." Lady Langford glanced up from the letter. "I do not know of this Lord Linwood. However, I am familiar with Sir Christopher."

"Is he someone of importance?" Frances had never heard his name mentioned before.

"He is half-brother to Miss Victoria Abbott," Lord Langford told his daughter.

"And who is Miss Victoria Abbott?" The two young ladies shared the same surname and one could make the assumption.... Was she truly related to Frances?

"She is your first cousin," said her father. "Victoria is my younger brother, John's, girl."

"My cousin?" This could not be the first Frances had heard the name. "How is it I do not know of her?"

"Because, my dear, we do not speak of her," her mother stated rather stiffly.

"As my brother is no longer with us and his offspring reside with their mother. Miss Abbott's mother has remarried a number of times and I cannot think what she is presently called."

"*Lady Yardley Grayson.*" Lady Langford drew in a breath before stating, "Miss Victoria Abbott is sister to John, heir presumptive of the Langford earldom."

"But what does this duel have anything to do with my engagement to Sir Russell?" Frances did not wish to appear self-centered or childish, even if it was only before her parents, but the actions of all those strangers could not have anything to do with her, with her life.

"It is the horrid scandal of the duel, my dear."

"That has nothing to do with me...us...our family, can it?" Frances still did not understand what had happened to bring this about.

"Unfortunately, we *are* connected to them. They *are* our family." Lady Langford's sorrow got the best of her and she began to weep. One of her delicate silk handkerchiefs appeared in her hand and she pressed it to her eyes. "This is too terrible."

"But I have done nothing—" Frances, who felt glorious dressed in one of her new gowns, an ivory confection with Pompeian red and gold trim, now felt her eyes well up with tears. She had no wish to be a watering pot but she could not help it. "I have never met, nor had I known of, my *cousin* Victoria...or her brother John, or of Sir Christopher Glory. I have never heard of any of them, yet I must suffer his—her behavior? Why? This is not...not fair."

"There is nothing *fair* about this, my sweet," her father tried to calm her. "It is the way the world works."

"But it is *not* fair!" Frances refused one of her mother's handkerchiefs. She did not care if her tears streamed down her face or onto her gown.

Lord Langford's voice grew stern. "Frances, regardless of this broken engagement you must make the best out of the next two months. I do not know if it is possible for you to return next year."

"For a *third* Season? Impossible!" Lady Langford cried out very near hysterics now. "Never say so, my lord!"

"How am I to prevent any of this?" Frances, who by now, believed herself to be the unluckiest female in England. Two broken engagements, neither of which was her fault.

"Of course, we still must attend the rout tonight." Lady Langford gestured to their evening finery with a sweep of her hand. "We simply cannot abandon Lady Bridgeport. It is too late to send regrets. We must make an appearance."

"Am I expected to attend and pretend nothing has happened?" Frances could not control the quaver in her voice any more than she could prevent the tears from streaking down her face.

"Of course," her mother replied. "No one knows of the match between you and Sir Russell. You must go on as you normally would."

"Very well. I will go. Please, Mama, let us not stay long. I do not think I can...."

"I understand, my dear. I understand." Lady Langford sniffed one last time, blotted her nose, and gave Frances' arm a little squeeze and with a weak smile said, "I am sure all will be well."

At just before seven that evening, Pauline, already dressed for dinner in a pale blue gown, waited for her mother on the third story landing.

Mrs. Chandler approached her daughter while shaking her head. "He refuses to join us," she whispered, sounding more cross than sympathetic to her son's plight, and began to descend the staircase.

"You cannot blame him, Mama. Martin must be absolutely heartbroken." Pauline followed her mother down the stairs.

"I do not understand why he cannot put his melancholy aside to dine with our guests."

"He needs time, Mama." Pauline did not know precisely what had happened to cause his broken engagement. Perhaps no one knew except for Victoria and Martin themselves. Until he decided it was time to confide in his family it would continue to be a mystery and plague them.

"He would forget all about Victoria if he had a mind."

"It is far too soon, I think. One cannot simply *forget* someone they love." *She* could not, at least. Pauline paused on the stairwell feeling her words quite deeply. Surely Martin felt the same.

Pauline had never been in love with anyone before so she did not exactly know. Her heart ached for her brother all the same. She gazed up in the direction of his room and hoped he was not permanently injured by his recent heartbreak.

"It does not do to go on about Martin's situation." Mrs. Chandler motioned that Pauline should move along. "Come now, we will soon have guest. You may welcome Jane and Mrs. Heffelfinger."

Pauline continued her descent. "Victoria might have called him a *coward* for not insisting he take part in the duel. Perhaps she told him as much to his face!"

They had been told that Sir Christopher, as Victoria's brother, had every right to uphold his sister's honor. Perhaps Martin could have insisted he face Lord Linwood.

Mrs. Chandler did not wait for her daughter and moved down the staircase. "We do not even know what has happened between Victoria and Martin. Why do you insist on speculating?"

"There could have been a horrid row!" Pauline paused on the second floor landing and her hand came to her cheek to rest. "Oh, that would have been dreadful!"

"Pauline, dear," Mrs. Chandler, arriving on the first floor, turned back to the staircase to address her daughter. "You know nothing of the sort. Please do not create a situation where your brother is cast as the tragic hero."

"*Tragic hero*, indeed, ma'am." Pauline could not understand how her mother could be so unfeeling regarding her own offspring.

Mrs. Chandler stepped onto the ground floor just as a footman opened the front door. "There you are!" She welcomed the dinner guests with a smile.

"Good evening, Mrs. Chandler." Mrs. Heffelfinger followed Jane into the house.

"Pauline asks that you excuse her for not welcoming you herself. She will be down in a moment." Mrs. Chandler stepped to one side to make room for the guests.

"I did not see Pauline peer out the window." Jane looked

about, somewhat quizzically. "How did she know we had arrived and not your other guests?"

"Because Jane, I knew it must have been you." Pauline stepped into the foyer. "For as long as I have known her, Lady Emmeline has always been the last to arrive at every gathering."

Mrs. Chandler rested her hand on her chin in thought. "That cannot be so."

Jane unfastened her pelisse and pulled loose the ribbon to her bonnet. "Oh, surely not." She removed her bonnet and handed it to her aunt.

"How well you look this evening, Jane." Pauline greatly admired her friend's primrose yellow gown. The soft ruffles barely brushed the floor. She linked Jane's arm through her own and led her friend to the front parlor, leaving her mother and Mrs. Heffelfinger to hand off the outerwear to the footman.

"Thank you." Jane fell in step next to Pauline. "Does Lady Emmeline know my aunt and I are to attend this evening?"

"I do not believe so," Pauline replied. "Your presence will certainly be a surprise for them."

"Then how could she know to delay her arrival if she had no knowledge that we were invited?" Jane sat on the sofa and Pauline sat next to her.

"I have no idea but she is very clever, among other things." Pauline was not altogether certain it was possible to quantify and contrast the qualities of Lady Emmeline.

"Do tell me a bit more about her, if you please." Jane gazed at her friend, eager for her next words.

"Well...I have been acquainted with Lady Emmeline Cordia-Darling for a very long time. Our mothers attended school together and have since remained good friends. They frequently write to one another. I do not know Lady Emmeline well, for we were only children when we first met and have been in each other's company a handful of times, but now she has come to Town for her first Season."

"Will she take, do you think?" It was a common concern for all young ladies, and their mothers.

"Oh, yes," Pauline stated with certainty. "She is the daughter of the Earl and Countess of Kennington. I'm sure she has a handsome dowry. She is very pretty and has lovely brown hair and eyes and is everything that is admirable and quite accomplished. She plays the pianoforte with masterful skill and sings exceptionally well. I cannot help but think gentlemen will all find her most charming."

"I see." Jane glanced down at her clasped hands resting in her lap. "I wonder if I will ever have such an effect on the opposite sex."

"Oh, Jane, you and I are both too young to think of suitors and such." Their untimely presence in London during the Season was only for the occasion of their sibling's nuptials. Thank goodness they had the friendship of each other.

"I suppose you're right." Jane sighed. "One cannot help but think of such things when it is going on all around." Did she not consider herself pretty enough? Jane had many accomplishments, not unlike Lady Emmeline.

"I agree wholeheartedly. There is nothing but talk of parties and eligible gentlemen and matches from all quarters."

Mrs. Chandler entered the parlor followed by Mrs. Heffelfinger.

"Where is Lady Kennington?" Mrs. Chandler murmured and wrung her hands. "It is nearly time to go in for dinner and she and Emmeline have yet to arrive."

"I'm sure they'll be here soon." Pauline moved to the double-sashed window and peered outside in time to see a crested coach come to a stop before the house. "I believe they are here now."

"Just in time! They will barely have time to say hello before we all need to remove to the dining room."

There was a commotion in front of the house and passengers disembarking from the coach. The voices were soft but clearly female. Mrs. Chandler swept into the foyer to greet her long-time friend. The butler opened the door.

"Ah, Isabelle! You have finally come!" Mrs. Chandler called to the newcomers.

"Dear Mary!" The ladies clasped hands, leaned toward each other, and kissed both cheeks in greeting. Lady Kennington stepped away and gestured for her daughter to come forward. "You, of course, remember my dear Emmeline."

"Welcome, Lady Emmeline. How well you look, and what a beauty you have turned into!" Mrs. Chandler nodded to her friend. "She will certainly break some hearts this Season."

Lady Emmeline Cordia-Darling stepped into the foyer of the townhouse. Once her pelisse was removed one could see the soft peach color of her gown perfectly complementing her fine, clear complexion.

Jane gasped when observing the beautiful long-lashed, brown eyes of the newcomer as they followed the trail of small, decorative flowers flowing down from the waistline of her dress to the hem of her skirt. The earl's daughter lifted her gaze from the lovely detail of her dress and graced those around her with a warm smile.

It had been just over a year since Pauline had seen Lady Emmeline. In that short time she had blossomed. She seemed to glide without effort across the floor. Her hand and arm gestures appeared delicate and graceful.

"She is exquisite!" Jane whispered in reverent tones.

"Yes, she is quite changed from last I saw her," Pauline replied. "She is much improved. I did not think that would be possible."

"Pauline!" Lady Emmeline smiled and entered the parlor, approaching the two young ladies. "It has not been so long but I very nearly did not recognize you."

"It is so very good to see you." Pauline dipped a curtsey. "Lady Emmeline may I make you known to my friend Miss Jane Stiles."

"How do you do, Lady Emmeline?" Jane bowed her head.

"How do you do, Miss Stiles?" Lady Emmeline straightened. "I believe I have heard your name from one of Mrs. Chandler's many letters to my mother. You are the sister of Martin Chandler's fiancée Miss Abbott, are you not? I *am* so very delighted to meet you."

"I am astonished that you should in any way know of me." Jane smiled. "Pauline said you were pretty but, I never imagined...you are really quite beautiful."

"*Beautiful?*" A slight pink washed across Lady Emmeline's cheeks in a most becoming blush. She turned away with a sparkle in her eye and a flash of a dimple when she smiled. "Oh, please, do not tease me."

The devastatingly lovely image stunned Pauline. This was not the girl she remembered. Emmeline had always been pretty but this *creature*...was truly bewitching.

"Come, ladies," Mrs. Chandler called to the trio of young women in the parlor. "We are already late for dinner. If we are not seated now it will be ruined. Come along. Come at once!"

"Yes, Mrs. Chandler," Lady Emmeline returned. With a backward glance and a coy smile, she left.

Jane touched Pauline's arm to delay her friend for just a moment.

"Would it be terrible of me to say it is my most sincere desire that I resemble Lady Emmeline by the time I am to Come Out?"

Over an hour after arriving at the Bridgeport residence, Lady Frances Abbott, an obedient daughter, had done as her mother had asked. She displayed a smile and paid her respects to her hosts, greeted those guests she already knew, and made the acquaintance of many new to her. All with her social mask in place.

It was grossly unfair. Not merely that her engagement to Sir Russell had been called off, but other than her initial angry outburst, she was not allowed to...to even give a thought to what she truly felt. More than anything, Frances had not even a minute alone to herself since receiving her bad news.

When her mother was well-occupied with Lady Halford it was time for Frances to find a moment of solitude. Exiting the reception room, she was careful not to make eye contact with anyone and looked for a small, vacant room in which she could closet herself.

Making her way down the corridor, Frances heard the whispered name: *Sir Christopher Glory*, a person who had been only recently known to her and caused her to pause, slowing her progress. Curiosity caused her to linger to hear more of the gentlemen's conversation.

"Where is he?" She heard one man say. "Haven't seen him about."

"I certainly have not seen him here tonight," said another.

"I'm sure he hasn't run off. He's the victor!"

"Linwood's gone back to the country, you know," said a fourth, distinguished by a very low voice.

"Gad, did you hear? Sir Christopher spared the wretch's life."

"Deloped is what I heard."

Frances could no longer distinguish the men's voices and had no idea how many partook in the discussion.

"That's what I've heard-say as well."

"There was no shame in what he's done," the man with the low voice said.

"What shame? Noble, I'd say. A very noble act. He should be proud of himself for standing up for his family."

"It was a matter of honor, was it not?"

"I do believe it was...his sister's. She had been slighted. Terribly!"

"Linwood should count himself as lucky."

"As well he should. Glory had every right to shoot him through."

"He's an example for everyone."

"Yes, one must not allow anger to rule. One must make an intellectual decision about such things. We ain't animals!"

"Quite right, Clive. Quite right."

Frances had heard enough. It appeared there was a consensus that Sir Christopher Glory was a paragon among men. He probably had no knowledge of Frances and could not know how his actions had ruined her life.

She continued on her way to find some solitude.

There were very few people congregating beyond the three large reception rooms and she continued down the corridor to the right. Checking each room, she came upon a small sitting room with a cozy lit fire.

Finally! A place to sit and be quiet, alone with her thoughts.

Sitting near the fire, Frances closed her eyes and exhaled, giving herself permission to release whatever emotion she had suppressed to emerge. Whether it be immense grief, a bucketload of tears, wild, hysterical laughter, she would be free to express it.

It felt wonderful to sit and be alone with her thoughts. Frances allowed her false mask to fall away and whatever welled inside her to emerge. She waited, inhaled and exhaled again, and waited. And waited.

Nothing happened.

What did she feel? It seemed to her that sadness would be the most appropriate response. In truth, the emotions residing in Frances' heart was more akin to disappointment than sadness that her engagement had ended.

"I have found you!" Sir Russell Crawford stepped into the room and glanced over his shoulder before closing the door behind him. "And how fortunate for us that you are alone."

"Russell?" Frances shot to her feet upon his unexpected and sudden appearance. "What are you doing here?"

"*Fan*, dearest, please, I must speak to you." Dressed in a dark jacket and white pantaloons with an ornate waistcoat and splendidly crafted cravat, Sir Russell looked as though he had taken great pains to dress for the evening.

"You should not be here. We should not be together...alone." Frances slowly retook her seat albeit with trepidation. "Lady Emerson had written Mama that you were not to attend tonight."

"My mother may have changed her mind but she does not speak for me." He sat next to her, taking up her hand. "I want to reassure you that nothing between *us* has changed."

"Not changed?" Frances drew her hand from his. "Our engagement has ended."

"So say my parents but they will come 'round, you'll see," he said with certainty.

"I will not go against their decision. You should not ask it of me." She would not dare act against the wishes of their parents and could not imagine Russell asking her to defy them.

"There will be no need, my dear," Russell assured her. "We only have to be patient, just for a bit, all will be well."

"If what you say is true then...very well." Frances would have liked nothing better than to believe their engagement stood. But she could not quite feel comfortable about it.

However, if Russell insisted that Lord and Lady Emerson would, given time, change their minds, and all they needed to do was remain patient. She would be content to wait. However, her hopes were not high that any amount of time would change her situation.

four

PAULINE REALIZED THEIR DINING room was not bedecked in its most elegant finery. The table did not hold their best china nor the best silver that night. As her mother had informed her, and their guests earlier, the evening meal would be very casual, *en famille,* a gathering for a few friends, enjoying *comfortable* surroundings, not a fancy dinner party.

The ladies settled around the table, Mrs. Chandler at the head. Lady Kennington, Lady Emmeline sat to her right, and Jane, Mrs. Heffelfinger to her left. Pauline sat at the end, between the two younger ladies.

She glanced at the others around the table waiting for the soup service. The minutes stretched on. Everyone remained quiet until the servants retreated and Pauline took up her spoon.

"This is just the thing, a very comfortable coze among friends," Lady Kennington commented, approving the *ladies only* company. "I know how happy you were that Martin was finally to marry. I wish to offer my condolences regarding your son's broken engagement."

"Thank you, Isabelle." Mrs. Chandler returned a weak smile.

"I still have difficulty believing it has happened. It is most unfortunate. We still do not know *how* it has happened."

"How can that be?" Lady Kennington lowered her spoon, resting the handle on the edge of the bowl. "She cried off, did she not? It cannot be something your Martin has done."

"I truly do not know." The hostess blinked back the moisture welling in her eyes. "He has not told us exactly what has happened between them. I must say he did not appear to me to be overwrought by the incident."

"Men never are, my dear," Lady Kennington said in a knowing way. "If that is the case, it is a shame that Martin cannot join us this evening. I'm sure he would find our company vastly amusing."

"No, I'm afraid not." The emotional wave that Mrs. Chandler moments ago had subsided. "I'm afraid he cannot be persuaded to leave his rooms."

"Your brother is here, in this house, and he keeps to his rooms while there are guests?" Lady Emmeline sounded quite indignant.

"We cannot know how he is feeling. I'm sure he must be sad, perhaps disappointed. He must have had his heart broken and he could feel quite angry at the outcome." Jane interjected cautiously. "My sister Victoria can be quite...ill-tempered and quarrelsome at times."

Pauline heard Lady Emmeline utter a soft, "*Rude!*"

Clearly, the comment was not meant for anyone's ears for she looked to no one for a response, nor did anyone look to her in regard to her outburst.

"I can only imagine that he could have been terribly hurt by what went on between them or perhaps what Victoria might have said," Jane continued. "His family must treat him with care and kindness during this time. When he is ready to face Society once again he can rest assured that we will all welcome him upon his return."

"And what of your sister, Miss Stiles?" Lady Emmeline, with a voice of calm, asked. "Has *Victoria* isolated herself to recover? Can she bear the company of others around her?"

"No, she has been exiled." Jane cast her gaze downward. She felt a bit shy about the resolution. "Our brother is at this moment escorting her and our mother to Bath to wait out the remainder of the Season."

Lady Kennington covered her mouth to staunch her gasp and shook her head in disbelief. "Bath? That is harsh, just as the Season begins."

"Victoria has done something very bad to warrant such treatment." Jane sounded very sad, taking her sister's punishment to heart. Clearly, it affected her greatly.

"What a dreadful—" Lady Emmeline moaned. "Whilst I believe her punishment must have been warranted...but *Bath?* I cannot conceive of a more dreadful consequence."

"Is your brother to remain her keeper?" Lady Kennington's inquiry was becoming uncomfortable. Her acquaintance with Jane was too new to make such questions about her family and their whereabouts acceptable.

"He cannot. Sir Christopher is to return by the end of the week." Mrs. Heffelfinger turned to Jane. "I think we have said enough, dear."

"Yes, of course." Jane glanced at Pauline. As shocked as they were, the silent communication between them spoke of the knowledge of the duel that had taken place early that morning.

Did Lady Emmeline and her mother know?

RUSSELL RELUCTANTLY STEPPED OUT OF THE ROOM AND CLOSED the door behind him. The last thing he wanted was to leave Frances' side but he had not wished to have her compromised by being found alone with her behind a closed door. He couldn't do that to her.

It would be impossible to remain under the same roof and not share her company or gaze upon her. He had to leave the house so he would not be tempted.

Arriving at Brooks, Russell handed his hat and gloves to the footman and headed down the corridor toward the lounge when he came across Lord James Dawson and Richard Harriot.

"Crawford!" one man called out, another shouted, "Russell Crawford!"

"Harriot! Dawson!" Russell returned.

"What are you doing in Town, old man?" Lord James led Harriot to Russell's side and was the first to shake his hand.

"Back in the petticoat line this Season?" Harriot ventured.

Russell shrugged. He was not yet officially engaged as far as his friends knew. He would not divulge that he had already found his heart's desire and would not be seeking a wife.

"We were going in for a drink. Won't you join us?" Lord James motioned toward the interior of the club.

"I can think of nothing I'd rather do. Thank you." Russell welcomed this distraction. More than just a way to pass some time, perhaps he could learn something of the duel his mother spoke of this morning.

"Lead the way, won't you, Harriot?" Lord James motioned for Russell to follow their friend. Up the staircase, the men climbed and walked down the long corridor towards the rooms that were the farthest away, which the older members did not care to inhabit.

"In here." After ducking his head around two open doors,

Harriot entered the third. Russell and Sir James followed. The pair glanced around the empty room and settled onto two of the club chairs next to the warm hearth. Sir James tugged the bellpull for a footman before taking his seat.

Harriot pulled out a cheroot from a case in his jacket. He stepped toward one of the side tables to use the flame from the small candelabra to light the end.

A footman arrived at the same time Harriot lowered into the vacant chair near Russell and Lord James.

"Bring a bottle, will you?" Lord James glanced at the other two, who both nodded then addressed the footman. "And three glasses."

The three sat in silence for a few minutes, enough time to assure they would be private, as private as one could be here.

"You're turned out smart, Crawford." Lord James crossed his legs while eyeing Russell.

"Bang up to the mark, I'd say." Harriot exhaled, blowing a cloud of smoke. "Been making the rounds tonight?"

"Made an appearance at the Bridgeport's," Russell replied. It wasn't some secret he was trying to keep.

"We all must *do the pretty* every now and again. Can't be helped." Lord James followed this with a roll of his eyes. "My mother will be on me to find a bride this Season."

"Will she?" Harriot sounded a bit taken aback. "I thought you were in no great hurry."

"I ain't. It's my mum." Lord James reached out, almost behind him, snagging a glass off the tray as the footman passed. "Come on, be quick with it, will you?" He urged the servant.

Sir James' glass was the first to be filled, and first to be drained, and refilled. Russell and Harriot waited patiently for theirs.

"I don't know how long I can put her off."

"I don't expect it would hurt to stand in the petticoat line and *look*, that should please her." Harriot held his glass in one hand and his cheroot in the other, alternating his vices.

"Mothers always try to *mother* regardless of your age," Russell added, speaking from experience. "One simply has to think a few steps ahead."

"I suppose so." In another swallow, Lord James had drained his glass. He left his chair to find the bottle.

"We're grown men, after all." Russell glanced at Harriot, not so much for reassurance, more to take in the adult Richard Harriot. All he needed was a lady-bird on his knee and a deck of cards in front of him to complete the picture.

"Yes, we are!" Harriot raised his glass, saluting Russell.

"Don't matter—Season's started off wretched." Lord James shook his head.

Russell would have to agree. He thought he would share his beloved's company about Town before their wedding. Instead, they were apart and his plans for marriage were...he didn't want to think about it. As far as he was concerned *wretched* was an apt description.

"M'brother's been a second for Linwood this morning." He gestured with his arm holding his recently filled glass, sending the contents running over the rim. "This morning!"

"A duel, you say?" This caught Russell's attention. What were the chances this was the same duel that had altered his life?

"That's famous! I haven't heard of it yet. Tell us, James." Harriot sat forward, appearing anxious for the news.

"Not much to tell, really." Lord James drained half his glass. "Charles tried talking to both Linwood and Sir Christopher Glory" —the remaining liquid disappeared— "Didn't do any good, Linwood slighted Sir Christopher's sister."

"Don't know him personally but it's understandable, one has

to be ready to die for one's family honor," Harriot replied. "I'm sure I would if I had any sisters."

"No harm done, though. No one's hurt." Lord James brought his glass to his lips but found it empty. "Charles said Linwood's dashed off to the family pile in Kent."

"And what of Sir Christopher?" Of course, Russell was more than slightly interested but did not let on.

"No idea. I'm afraid I've never had the pleasure. Don't know anyone who knows him, really." Lord James shrugged.

"So the Season starts with a duel, chances are the nonsense is over with and we can go on about our business. Here, here!" Harriot raised his glass ending his toast.

Russell joined in. "Well said!"

"Hang on." Lord James, discovering his glass was empty, stood, and headed toward the bottle for another refill. "We'll need a new bottle before we can drink to the end of duels."

JANE HATED TO THINK ILL OF HER NEW ACQUAINTANCE, ESPECIALLY when she thought the earl's daughter so very beautiful and had every wish to emulate her. There really was no other explanation for her to behave in what Jane would consider a *gauche* manner. It was as if Lady Emmeline was purposefully driving a wedge between her and Pauline.

"How awkward this must be for the two of you." Lady Emmeline looked from Jane to Pauline after the removal of soup and the arrival of the next course. "The engagement between your siblings has ended and yet you sit here sharing an enjoyable meal."

"It is true our families were brought together by Martin and Victoria's engagement but there is no reason why our friendships should suffer because they do not marry." Pauline replaced the spoon after serving herself peas.

"I am quite certain that Sir Christopher and Mr. Chandler will remain the best of friends," Mrs. Heffelfinger added. "His decision to move Miss Victoria to Bath may have been a way to preserve the harmony between the families."

"That is very true, Mrs. Heffelfinger." Mrs. Chandler pushed a slice of beef to one side of her plate with her fork. "It is a fact that Martin thinks highly of Sir Christopher, and I do not see how even a broken engagement would change that."

"I hate to say this of my own sister but Victoria's absence certainly makes our lives more agreeable," Jane confessed.

"As to that...I have just had a thought." Lady Kennington drew the attention of those around the table. "Emmeline and I were planning a short shopping outing tomorrow morning. Since you, Miss Stiles, and Mrs. Heffelfinger are without a proper escort, why not join us? And dearest Mary, why don't we make a party of it? Shall we all go together?"

"That would be famous!" Lady Emmeline cheered.

"We could all meet here," Mrs. Chandler continued.

"It might be a sad crush but the six of us could fit in our coach. It is only a short way to Bond Street," Lady Kennington announced with optimistic glee.

"That sounds splendid." Jane must have been mistaken about her ladyship and her daughter. They were quite welcoming with their offer to share their shopping expedition.

Of course, Jane had no need for dresses, gloves, or any other fripperies but the opportunity to go about Town was not to be missed. She thought it might be great fun.

"And we shall all sit for a nice tea when we return," Mrs. Chandler added.

Pauline laughed and glanced at Jane and Lady Emmeline.

She shared Jane's delight regarding their outing. Lady Emmeline appeared to be quite pleased with the plans as well.

"That is excellent, ladies. I do thank you for including us," Mrs. Heffelfinger replied.

"Then it's all settled. Shall we meet here, let's say...at ten?" Lady Kennington suggested.

"Now that we have our arrangements for tomorrow laid out before us, let us finish our meal and we can remove to the parlor," Mrs. Chandler said. "I believe a rubber or two of Whist will be a splendid finish to this evening if we can convince one of the young ladies to make our four."

"I beg your pardon, Mrs. Chandler," Lady Emmeline was quick to answer. "The three of us already have agreed that we should play Speculation."

"I abhor Speculation!" Lady Kennington visibly shuddered.

"I know, Mama, that is why I, above all, wish to play because I never have a chance at home."

That was an outright lie. Jane and Pauline had made no such agreement with Lady Emmeline regarding card play.

"No matter, Mary, the three of us shall make do with Piquet," Lady Kennington reassured her friend.

"It matters not what we play, Isabelle. Truly."

"If Mrs. Peckover had accompanied us we would have had a foursome for Whist, however, I saw no need for a chaperone this evening. Had I known...."

"You had no knowledge others were invited to join us." With a sigh of regret, Mrs. Chandler set her fork on her plate and motioned for the servants to bring the final course.

At the end of the meal, before the elder ladies left the dining room for the parlor, Lady Emmeline urged Jane and Pauline to quickly depart while the older ladies dallied about the table doing who-knows-what.

"I am sorry I told my mother we had already decided on Speculation when we had done no such thing." She shook her head. "If I hadn't they would have pulled us into their circle and there would not have been a moment's peace for any of us."

"That's quite clever of you, Lady Emmeline," Pauline replied.

"It's not to avoid *your* mother but *my* mother." Lady Emmeline stated quite strongly. "She cannot help it but I have learned a few tricks to escape her clutches."

Clutches? Jane could not help but giggle.

"If you only knew...." Lady Emmeline gave an exasperated sigh. "My mother means well, of course, but—"

"Your mother *always* gets her way," Pauline supplied, in case there was any doubt.

"How very true." Lady Emmeline urged the other two down the corridor, returning to the parlor. "You should thank me, Miss Stiles."

Actually, Jane felt relieved that there was no malice in Lady Emmeline's heart by the small deception. Why had Jane taken the notion the newcomer was up to some mischief?

"I expect the older ladies will take their place at the table over there. They will want to be seated where it is warm." Lady Emmeline indicated the sturdy table across the room to one side of the hearth. "Where shall we sit?"

"A good-ways from their table, I should think." Pauline called a footman to move a table out from the wall and a second who drew up an extra chair for Jane.

"That should do very well for us, don't you think?" Lady Emmeline sat in one of the seats and motioned for Jane and Pauline to take the others.

Lady Emmeline shuffled the cards before going around and around dealing many cards face down on the table.

"Three cards, *Em*," Pauline whispered, reminding the dealer, while she was busy passing out the gaming fish.

"Oh, yes, I remember. How silly of me." She retrieved the extra cards mistakenly dealt and turned the next card from the deck to determine trump.

Jane and Pauline took up their cards and placed them in order.

"Why, you are not interested in playing Speculation after all." Jane came to the realization after noticing that Lady Emmeline's attention was not intent on the cards she held in her hand.

"I'm afraid not." She appeared a bit guilty. "Since we cannot be overheard, I thought we might share some gossip. What shall we talk about?"

"Gossip?" This was a new game for Jane. "We have not been in Town for long and we are not acquainted with many people."

"Perhaps I should be the one telling you the latest *on dit*." Lady Emmeline tucked her arms close to her body and leaned forward.

"Oh, yes, please," Pauline responded wide-eyed, sounding very curious. "Do, please do, tell us."

"Well, we must keep up the pretense that we are occupied in our game." Lady Emmeline informed them. "My mother will undoubtedly grow suspicious."

"Of course, we shall continue." Jane glanced in the direction of the older ladies. She did not wish to miss a single forthcoming word. Pauline made a show of reordering cards in her hand.

"Whilst I do not believe I have met any of these people as of yet," Lady Emmeline began, "I understand that when *these* types of stories are relayed that names are not mentioned."

With a glance, Jane and Pauline silently agreed, understanding the need for anonymity. Jane moved her cards about before leaning closer to listen.

Lady Emmeline's voice softened. "I have been told that there is a Miss D— who has not been circumspect in her affections toward a certain Lord H—" She elongated the surname initials to create a bit of suspense. "The Season has yet to begin and I hear they are making cakes of themselves over one another."

"Really?" Pauline appeared to be intrigued by the news. "Are they so openly attached?"

"No one would dare declare affection for another when the Season has yet to begin," Lady Emmeline went on. "What fun would that be?"

Pauline and Jane gazed wide-eyed and both held back their gasps lest they let it be known they were not in the midst of their game but busy gossiping.

"But there must be many Miss Ds and several Lord Hs in Town," Jane could not help but wonder aloud.

"How is one to know the identities of these persons?" Pauline whispered.

"*One* doesn't—" Lady Emmeline remarked. "That is half the fun! Every Miss D and Lord H *one* comes across will leave *one* to wonder."

The three sat back in their chairs and studied their cards or made to look as if they were doing so. Pauline glanced at the table near the hearth where the older ladies sat to check if they suspected the younger ladies were not playing.

"Allow me to relay another." Lady Emmeline's gaze shifted from the older ladies back to Jane and Pauline. "There is a Lady F— who has ended her lengthy engagement to Lord A— and has returned for a second Season. I hear that she need not bother because she already has a beau-in-waiting to wed her."

"Already?" Jane wondered at having several gentlemen in

line for one's attention. She felt lucky if she could have one beau. Lady Emmeline, of course, would have many. She really was beautiful and Jane felt very small and mousey in comparison.

"I have also heard there is a certain gentleman who is trying to make a fashion statement and Beau Brummell has not decided if it should be adopted or not."

"Who is Beau Brummell?" Pauline stared at Jane to see if she knew but her vacant expression said that she had no idea.

"Mr. George Byron Brummell," Lady Emmeline began, "is the current arbiter of fashion and has established the male mode of dress."

"Have you young ladies forgotten the game rules?" Mrs. Chandler called to them over her shoulder.

"No, ma'am. We're just chatting between rounds," Lady Emmeline was quick to answer.

Jane could honestly say she had never met anyone more clever. Lady Emmeline was ever-so patient and made explanations when needed. Jane and Pauline knew nothing of the ways of London.

"I expect you two will soon be picking up bits of gossip once you circulate around Town. There will be so many people about. I daresay most may have yet to arrive."

How did Lady Emmeline hear such things? She must have already attended some pre-Season parties. It seemed to Jane that the earl's daughter knew everyone.... At least, quite a lot of people.

However, she had no knowledge of her brother's duel that morning. And Jane had no doubt it wouldn't be long until she found out.

Would she be angry with Jane or Pauline that they did not

tell the one piece of gossip they knew? Even if it implicated their families in what she would consider a delicious scandal.

five

JANE WOKE EARLY THE next morning, knowing she needed to arrive at the Chandlers' before ten, and took breakfast alone in the morning room. Grayson House was far too quiet without the presence of her mother, brother, and sister. Her life was not bereft of company. She had a splendid time playing Speculation last night and participating in the gossip after dinner. How nice it was to make the acquaintance of Lady Kennington and her daughter Lady Emmeline Cordia-Darling.

However at the moment, none of that mattered...Jane pined for her own family.

"You look so very sad, my dear." Mrs. Heffelfinger entered the breakfast room carrying her shawl, hat, and reticule.

"Is it time to leave?" Exactly how long had Jane been sitting there? She lowered her cup to its saucer. It seemed to her she woke a mere hour or so before.

"Not quite yet. You needn't rush." Mrs. Heffelfinger perused the breakfast offerings on the sideboard. "I was just pondering a last cup of coffee. However, it may not be the best decision when we are about to depart."

"Do sit here, next to me, Auntie." Jane brightened. "I thought perhaps I might find a bit of trim for one of my dresses or hats this morning, if that is acceptable."

"You should purchase it, by all means." Mrs. Heffelfinger finished filling a cup for herself and headed to the table. "I have some pin money for just the thing."

"I'm bringing some as well. I do not think it will do to buy on credit and leave it for Kit to settle when he returns."

"Oh, no!" Mrs. Heffelfinger's voice quavered in mock-horror. "That would not do. I'm sure he will not be thanking us for that."

"No, I wouldn't think so." Jane stared into her chocolate. Her brother was more than tolerant when it came to indulging her, but to presume such might not be acceptable.

"I beg your pardon, ladies." Liddell appeared at the breakfast room door. He subsequently entered, moved to Mrs. Heffelfinger's side, and lowered his silver salver.

She lifted the card to regard it and her eyebrows drew slightly upward. *Lady Langford...Lady Frances Abbott.*

"Her ladyship said this was regarding an extremely urgent matter." The butler conveyed in a calm that was, most probably, not near the *urgent* nature she must have implied.

"*Abbott....*" Mrs. Heffelfinger whispered. "A relation, do you think?"

Liddell's face remained impassive. "She asked for Sir Christopher and I informed her that he is not At Home. She insists she speak to *someone.*"

"I wonder why...." Mrs. Heffelfinger's eyes narrowed. Had she anticipated something nefarious?

"We cannot possibly have any answers to any questions she might ask, Aunt." Jane was uncertain as to what they should do.

"No, not regarding *that*, however, we could inform her as to the family's absence."

Her aunt was correct. To turn their visitors away without any explanation would be too unkind.

"They must be *relatives*, perhaps not ours *directly* but we cannot refuse them. Your mother would certainly welcome them if she were here."

"I'm sure you are right, Auntie." Jane stood slowly, readying herself for the encounter. "And so must we." She addressed the butler. "Show our guests into the front parlor, Liddell, if you please."

Mrs. Heffelfinger left her coffee and followed Jane out of the breakfast room door, down the corridor to the parlor.

"Welcome, Lady Langford." Mrs. Heffelfinger made a shallow curtsey to the countess.

"Please allow me to make us known to you, Lady Langford." Jane inclined her head showing due respect. "I am Sir Christopher's sister, Miss Stiles. This is my aunt, Mrs. Heffelfinger."

"Ladies, my daughter, Lady Frances Abbott." Lady Langford concluded the introductions.

"How do you do? Miss Stiles, Mrs. Heffelfinger." Lady Frances curtsied.

"How do you do, Lady Frances? Please be seated, won't you?" Mrs. Heffelfinger indicated the sofa with a gracious wave.

"Thank you," said Lady Langford. She lowered herself, not to sit but to perch, on the edge of the sofa. "I beg you ladies forgive the impropriety of our call. This is quite beyond the pale since I do not believe we share the slightest acquaintance." Lady Langford spoke with authority and slight discomfort.

"If I am not mistaken, your family must be connected to my half-sister Miss Victoria Abbott." Jane added hoping to make their unusual situation, somewhat-related yet total strangers acceptable to their visitors. For speaking openly, such as they were, was certainly not the thing.

Lady Langford's disagreeable reaction was palpable. Whether it was Jane's forthright speaking or the mention of Victoria's name, she could not be certain.

"You are correct, Miss Stiles. We are related to your sister. Miss Abbott and her younger brother John are Frances' first cousins. Young Mr. Abbott is also heir presumptive to the Langford earldom."

It was no wonder Lady Langford had called. Her family must have heard of the morning's incident and came to ring a peal over Kit's head for his involvement. It was astonishing to Jane just how many lives were affected by one duel.

"I believe an explanation regarding Sir Christopher's whereabouts are in order," Mrs. Heffelfinger offered.

"I should say so." Lady Langford appeared to be more at ease. Perhaps knowing she would have some answers brought her some relief. Lady Frances finally seated herself on the sofa next to her mother appearing equally uncomfortable as the rest of them.

Jane detected the tightness around Lady Frances' mouth and the manner in which she struggled to keep her chin elevated. She was doing her best to remain brave as well.

"Sir Christopher is currently ensuring Miss Victoria and Lady Yardley's safe passage to Bath."

"He's left Town?" Lady Langford renewed her grip on her reticule with some firmness, displaying her displeasure. "Does he think he can avoid scandal by leaving Town?"

"He did not leave for *his* benefit but for the families'. I am sure it would have generated some *talk*." Mrs. Heffelfinger shook her head as if she were chasing away any trace of lingering scandal. "He believes it best she remain in Bath for the remainder of the Season."

"That may be very well for him but the damage has already been done."

"Damage?" Mrs. Heffelfinger replied, as neither of them knew to what Lady Langford referred.

"His actions have brought Lady Frances' impending betrothal to an end." Her ladyship tilted her chin up, holding her head high. "It is due to no fault of hers yet she suffers the repercussions."

"It seems that she is among several others who have been unfortunately affected," Jane was quick to add.

"What would you have Sir Christopher do, may I ask?" Mrs. Heffelfinger continued. "He is currently caring for his own family. I am sure he would not willingly wish yours harm."

"Nor will he care, I own." Lady Langford stood. Lady Frances did the same.

"He's not as heartless as that." Jane would not tolerate any derogatory comments about her dear Kit. "All I can do is promise to relay your concerns to him upon his return, Lady Langford. I'm certain you will hear from him soon."

"Soon? Is that all you can offer?"

"In regards to your situation I know nothing, my lady, therefore I can offer nothing. I do know my brother and he is not one to shirk his duty, especially his family duty. You may not consider him as a relation but I assure you...he considers you part of his family."

"Very well, I await word of his return." With that Lady Langford and Lady Frances departed.

Jane and her aunt exchanged glances and said nothing more.

"I HOPE WE HAVE NOT ARRIVED TOO LATE!" MRS. HEFFELFINGER was quite out of breath upon entering the Chandler residence.

"No, no, Mrs. H. Never worry, you shan't be the last to arrive." Pauline met the guests in the foyer. "Might as well remove your outerwear and have some tea while we wait. Mama has already sent for a tray."

"Wait?" The chaperone flustered about a bit confused. "I thought we'd be late for certain."

Jane met Pauline's mirthful expression with one of her own. "It will be some time before Lady Emmeline and her mother arrive. You might as well make yourselves comfortable."

"You really are too cruel to say such a thing, Pauline." Jane unfastened her pelisse and handed it to a footman. She set her reticule and gloves on the table next to Pauline's own.

"It would only be cruel if it were not true." Pauline drew her giggling friend from the foyer.

"You are usually not this harsh." Jane allowed herself to be led into the parlor.

"You will soon see for yourself, Jane. The Beautiful Creature is most agreeable but she is forever tardy. Let us go inside and be seated."

Four teacups and saucers waited on the table. Pauline's mother and Mrs Heffelfinger were nowhere to be seen.

"Where is your mother?" Jane glanced about the room.

"And we've lost Mrs. H as well. We'll not wait for them," announced Pauline. "Allow me to pour."

"You are not willing to be patient for anyone today, are you?"

"The tea is hot and I abhor it cold or even at room temperature." Pauline filled two cups and replaced the teapot. "I must confess, I did enjoy Lady Emmeline's *gossip* last night."

"I did as well. I wish we knew some of those people, I'm certain it would make the stories far more interesting. Perhaps another few weeks in Town and we shall," Jane replied optimistically.

"Did you regret not relaying the account of Kit's duel?" Pauline imagined the juicy tidbits of a duel would trump the tale of Lady D, Lord H , Lady F and her new beau, or the Gentleman trying to usurp Beau Brummell's position as the leader of fashion. "If Lady Emmeline did not know, I'm certain she soon will."

"Oh, no." Jane grew serious. "I find nothing entertaining about Kit's participation. Just thinking about him with a firearm —having one aimed at him— The very thought terrifies me."

"But it's all over now and he is well. Actually all the participants emerged unharmed."

"Unharmed?" Jane set her cup and saucer on the table. "How can you say that? Victoria has been banished to Bath and your brother has locked himself in his room for who knows how long."

"Martin chooses to isolate himself. I'll not be fussed about his predicament. He is free to emerge whenever he likes."

"But his heart has been broken. Come now, Pauline. Do you not feel any sympathy for your brother?" Jane stared at her friend longing for some understanding.

Pauline wasn't sure she could empathize with Martin. "Don't we all have our hearts broken at some time or other?"

"Must we? I haven't...yet," Jane confessed. "But we are still young. I'm not looking forward to it."

"Then you must never fall in love and it will not happen." Pauline presumed that would be an unfailing method to ensure the safety of one's heart.

"Oh, dear...." Jane gasped.

"What is it?"

"I only just now recalled another casualty, perhaps it is two, who have been harmed by Kit's duel."

"Really?" Pauline thought this bit of news might be as interesting as Lady Emmeline's *on dits*.

"Although it is not my story to tell. I...." Jane stared at her friend wide-eyed in uncertainty. "Perhaps I should keep it to myself but you are my closest friend."

"I shan't tell Lady Emmeline, if that's your concern. I shan't tell anyone, if you insist."

"I shall tell you but you cannot utter a word to anyone else."

"Of course." Pauline anxiously waited.

Jane glanced about making certain they were alone and she began. "Moments before Mrs. H and I were to leave on our way here, we had two callers. Actually the visitors wished to speak to Kit...."

AFTER HER AND HER MOTHER'S ARRIVAL, LADY EMMELINE CORDIA-Darling wandered from the back of the Conduit Street house where the Chandler family resided toward the front. Mrs. Chandler had called to Lady Kennington and her daughter as they stepped down from their coach and all three entered the house from the side door.

Em thought that odd. Once inside, her mother joined Mrs. Chandler and Mrs. Heffelfinger, whom she had met the night before. Soon after, they sent her to search for Miss Stiles and Pauline. One was not left to wander through other people's houses...alone.

She eventually reached the foyer to find it empty. Not quite empty but void of people. On the foyer table she saw several pairs of gloves resting next to their owners' respective reticules. Em guessed the larger bag belonged to Mrs. Heffelfinger and the two smaller ones belonged to Miss Stiles and Pauline.

Lifting one of the gloves, only one, Em tucked it out of the way, behind the last baluster of the staircase, leaving it as if it had fallen there by chance. It would be funny to watch the others in their confusion to find the missing mate.

Em straightened and glanced about the room making certain her mischief had not been seen. Behind the parlor doors were two young voices in gleeful conversation.

"I beg your pardon...." Em leaned into the room uninvited. "I had hoped to find—"

"Em-meline!" Miss Stiles and Pauline called out and rushed toward her.

"You're finally here!" Pauline motioned that they should gather in the foyer. "We've been in the parlor waiting for you."

"*Waiting*? I have been wandering about the house for at least twenty minutes." It vexed Em when people complained when she was only a few minutes late. For it could not have been more than a *few* minutes.

"How are you this morning, Lady Emmeline?" Miss Stiles was very kind to ask instead of making impolite accusations. "I am very much looking forward to our outing."

"I am as well, Miss Stiles. Thank you." Em thought that perhaps she preferred Miss Stiles' company over that of her longtime acquaintance Pauline Chandler. "Do you think we should be on our way?"

Mrs. Heffelfinger entered the foyer, headed to the table, and took up her reticule. It was right where she left it. "The coach is coming around and we'll be leaving in a bit. Come on, girls."

Pauline moved to the table. Miss Stiles slipped her hand through the strings of her reticule and worked on her first glove.

"Is something wrong, Pauline?"

"One of my gloves is missing." Pauline did a cursory search of the table area, stepping back to look and see if it had fallen somewhere under. "I'm certain I had both when I left my bedchamber."

"Perhaps you should run back and check?" Em suggested, sending her into a bit of panic. "You must hurry!"

"I don't know if...." Pauline headed for the stairs then paused and turned, looking over her shoulder. "Do you think—"

"There!" Miss Stiles cried. "It's just there!" She pointed near Pauline's feet.

"Well spotted, Miss Stiles!" Em praised her.

"I suppose it must have fallen while I was on my way down." Pauline retrieved her wayward glove and shook it as if to punish it for wandering from its mate.

Em smiled. She thought it very amusing.

Mrs. Chandler, Lady Langford, and Mrs. Heffelfinger swept into the room.

"Come along, girls, it's time to leave!" Mrs. Chandler announced as she passed them. A footman appeared and opened the door for the three older ladies who immediately vacated the house.

Six

JANE THOUGHT THE SHOPPING trip was such good fun. She even managed to find a length of trim to purchase.

"Do allow me to step away." Lady Emmeline murmured to those standing on either side of her. She finished placing her order with the clerk and Lady Kennington wished to add a few items before closing her bill.

Mrs. Chandler had bought a hat she fancied a few shops back. She also found new trimmings in this shop and stood busy with a clerk making her purchase.

"I daresay the shops will find their shelves empty after we have visited." Pauline's opinion of her party's economy was that they were a bit extravagant.

"We have not purchased every item in every shop," Lady Emmeline commented.

"No, but it wasn't for want of trying." Jane giggled.

"True, there are a few shops we missed," Pauline replied. "And we have not stepped foot inside a dressmaker as of yet."

"Oh, what a shambles we-ladies could cause in that establishment. The seamstresses would be up to their ears with work if our party should enter their shop." Lady Emmeline smiled. Did she harbor a bit of pleasure at the thought of causing a bit of chaos? "No other ladies in Town would be able to place orders for the next fortnight."

"And there is such a need for good seamstresses. I am glad to have Mrs. Peckover, she is quite handy with a needle to make small alterations. Whilst the existing pale blue edging on my gown is nice, the gold edging is far superior. I find the white gowns we must wear insipid." Lady Emmeline, who was nearly two years their senior, informed Jane and Pauline.

"*Must* we wear white?" Pauline, who did not have an older sister as to have known this fact, inquired.

"I do recall Victoria having several small missteps last year." Jane thought it was beyond comprehension that they both would suffer through the very same when they attended their first Season next year.

"I have several gowns made with different colored ribbons and trim on the edges. I hope I can have one ready to wear tonight. I've included a note in my purchase instructing Mrs. Peckover that she should replace the edging on my neckline and armbands straightaway."

"Mrs. Peckover is your chaperone, is she not?" Pauline recalled hearing the name previously mentioned, probably by her mother.

"Is she handy with a needle?" Jane, who had her aunt for instruction on how to mend or replace trim, lacked the knowledge of hired chaperones, as did Pauline.

"Mrs. Peckover has proven herself quite talented in many ways." Lady Emmeline appeared pleased. "She did wish to accompany us today but Mama did not think there was a need."

"Six females shopping and not a male in sight." Pauline

could not imagine a situation less in need of a chaperone. "No, there is no need, is there?"

"Mama has signaled to me that we should meet them outside." Lady Emmeline whispered to Jane and Pauline. "They will be along in a few minutes when they've concluded their transactions."

"I'm excited to move on to the next shop." Jane, who had not known what to expect at the beginning of this trip, had learned very quickly.

"Excuse us." Pauline had to move out of the way lest she run into new customers entering the shop.

"I do beg your pardon," two women replied, stepping past them in the opposite direction.

Pauline giggled at the mishap with Jane as they exited the shop. Only a moment later, Emmeline emerged.

"Goodness, it's such a crush!" Emmeline straightened her sleeves and smoothed her skirts.

The three did not quite tumble onto the street but there was some effort to find a place for them all to stand, soon there would be the three elder ladies joining them.

"Oh no!" Emmeline stepped behind Jane and Pauline and peered over their shoulders. "That's not *him*, is it?"

"Who?" Pauline glanced about trying to see the *him* to whom Emmeline referred.

"Em?" One of the young men called from across the street. "Is that you, Em?"

"It is! My odious brother." Emmeline did her best to try to evade her sibling's notice.

"Why do you not wish your brother to see you?" Jane did not

understand any better than Pauline. Why would one refuse to acknowledge one's own brother?

"He has become entirely tiresome since he's started Oxford this year...new wardrobe, same friends."

"Emmeline, that is too bad of you to say about your own brother." Pauline would certainly not say such about Martin.

"Ah! He's seen me. Now we're in for it." Emmeline clearly dreaded the meeting. "We'll never be rid of him."

"Will you introduce us?" Jane sounded eager at the idea of meeting young men closer to her own age.

Emmeline did not seem thrilled at the notion.

"Em, please." The young man encouraged her and motioned to the two young men who accompanied him to near. "If not for me, for the lads. It's our first visit to Town, our first official social Season."

"Nicky, really. Very well." Emmeline did the pretty. "This is my brother Nicholas, Viscount Epping...Miss Stiles and Miss Chandler."

"How do you do, Miss Stiles?" He made a gracious leg.

"How do you do, Lord Epping?" Jane smiled and curtsied.

Emmeline cringed. "I cannot stand to hear you called that."

"It is his title," Jane quite correctly pointed out.

"Miss Chandler. How do you do?"

"How do you do, Lord Epping?" Pauline noted the family resemblance and considered him quite as handsome as his sister was beautiful.

Lady Emmeline gave a most unladylike sigh and rolled her eyes.

"Ladies, these are my friends. Hal—er, Mr. Newbury and Sir John Wanstead."

"Sir John, Mr. Newbury...." Pauline and Jane greeted the young men.

The gentlemen made slow nods of their heads and touched the brims of their hats, greeting them.

"Miss Chandler, Miss Stiles." Sir John gazed at Jane, showing some interest. "Are you two young ladies Out yet?"

"No, they are not!" Mrs. Heffelfinger answered, appearing seemingly from out of nowhere along with Mrs. Chandler and Lady Kennington.

"Nicky!" Lady Kennington scolded her son. "This is most improper. One does not perform introductions on the street."

"I am sorry, Mama, but I was with my mates and we were passing by and Em was here—"

"Hush!" The countess silenced her son. "If you wish to hold a discussion with these young ladies you, and your friends, may join us for tea."

By the anxious glances the young men shared, it seemed they did wish it.

"You will find us at the Chandler's residence on Conduit Street."

"Yes, ma'am," her son replied at the same time his friends answered, "Thank you, my lady."

"I am ignorant as to the identities of these other two but I am willing to wait for a proper introduction in a drawing room. When should we expect these young men, Mrs. Chandler?"

"At three?" the hostess replied.

"And do not be late." Lady Kennington instructed before she motioned them away and punctuated her comment with a tolerant sigh.

"I REGRET WE STAYED OUT SO LONG, MARY." LADY KENNINGTON

removed her bonnet and gloves and left them on the table in the entrance hall of the Conduit Street house.

"If it were not for the book shop and the bakery...which *was* a complete necessity with the additional guests. We would have been home *hours* ago." Mrs. Chandler, feeling just as fatigued as her friend, removed her gloves with some effort.

"I'm sorry for that." A great sigh escaped her ladyship. "I have overstepped my boundaries by inviting my son and his friends to tea. It really isn't my place."

"Nonsense, Isabelle. You must think nothing of it." Mrs. Chandler reassured her friend, setting her own gloves next to her bonnet. "We'd already discussed having refreshments before you and Emmeline were to leave. And you've been so good as to purchase some biscuits and cakes to feed us all, even our additional guests."

"I was attempting to make amends for my family's intrusion into your house." Her ladyship shook her head in disbelief. "I don't know what could have possessed me to suggest such a thing. Introductions on the street, before a storefront is an outrage! My son—*my* son...."

"It is sometimes difficult to understand young men." Mrs. Chandler sympathized. "As you will notice with my Martin and he is several years older than your Nicholas."

"Do you mean to tell me that he will *never* outgrow that— that—what do you call that type of behavior?"

"Childishness? Impetuousness?" Mrs. Chandler suggested.

"Youthfulness? Impulsiveness?" Lady Kennington offered.

"I do not wish to contemplate those notions and you should not give it another thought." Mrs. Chandler motioned that they should continue.

"It is difficult being a mother to boys, is it not?" Lady Kennington exhaled, sounding quite exasperated.

"It is. I find girls so much more level-headed."

"Speaking of the girls...where have they gone? Did we not all enter at the same time?" After a visual sweep of the foyer she headed to the parlor, and with a wave of her hand motioned her friend to follow her. "I'm afraid I must sit this instant, Mary."

"I believe they're in the dining room making order out of the small cakes that were delivered. They were contemplating meeting the young men there instead of in the parlor because there are so many of them." Mrs. Chandler strolled past the corridor, looking down toward the dining room to catch sight of them.

"Oh, to be young, eh, Mary?" Lady Kennington sought the comfort of a sofa. "My feet will attest to my age."

"I never wish to return to those years—even with the tempting return of *young* feet." Mrs. Chandler strolled to the front-facing windows alert to any arriving visitors.

"What time is it? How long do we have to relax before we are inundated by those...*gentlemen*?"

Mrs. Chandler glanced at the rosewood mantel clock. "Not long, it's quarter to three now."

"If they are late, we should begin and give not another thought to those three simpletons," her ladyship groused.

"Perhaps you should abandon the young people and remain in the parlor where it is quiet," Mrs. Heffelfinger said from the parlor doors.

"That may be just the thing, Mrs. H. What an excellent idea!" Mrs. Chandler would gladly take the chaperone up on her offer. "If Mrs. Heffelfinger remains with the girls and their guests, the two of us may enjoy our tea in the parlor."

"I am happy to oblige, ladies." Mrs. Heffelfinger clasped her hands in front of her. "How shall we determine *when* they are late, if I may ask?"

Lady Kennington and Mrs. Chandler gazed at one another, considering the question.

"If the tea is luke-warm, then they are late," Lady Kennington proclaimed.

"If the teapot is empty when they arrive, then they are late," Mrs. Chandler stated.

"I say when we have eaten all the cakes, they are definitely too late." Mrs. Heffelfinger concluded and before leaving she informed them, "I'll have a tray sent in."

THE CACOPHONY IN THE FOYER COULD ONLY MEAN THE ARRIVAL OF the young men. There were to be only three but the sound suggested there were thrice as many.

"Gracious!" The commotion caused the handle of Lady Kennington's teacup to slip between her fingertips. The liquid within slid dangerously toward the edge but her ladyship's well-practiced composure and balance returned equilibrium to her beverage. "Why must they be so raucous?"

From the foyer, Pauline motioned to the front parlor. "Let us greet the ladies properly and then we can retreat into the dining room."

Pauline, Jane, and their newly arrived guests entered the parlor to greet Lady Kennington and Mrs. Chandler before removing to the dining room where they had preparations for their tea.

Mrs. Heffelfinger had the good sense to close the parlor doors on her way out when the young people departed.

"That felt more like an interrogation than an introduction," Henry Newbury remarked when he stepped out of the corridor.

"Your mother is most formidable, *Epp*." Sir John Wanstead mumbled. He adjusted his neckcloth. "No offense."

"None taken, but you best keep your unflattering view of my parent to yourself lest my sister hear you," Nicholas, Lord Epping warned his friend. "That would lower her opinion of you, and you wouldn't want that."

They all made their way into the dining room.

"Oh, no...." Sir John froze and he gazed at Lady Emmeline, his eyes widened. "I would never wish to— Wouldn't think to *offend*—"

Pauline turned to see what had caused this peculiar reaction and when she realized it was only that he had set eyes upon Emmeline, she understood completely. The exquisitely lovely Lady Emmeline stood framed before the dining room window. Appearing even more breathtaking than one should in a simple afternoon frock and left Sir John quite speechless.

She did not tempt the young men with a beckoning or coquettish glance, Emmeline merely gazed across the room. When she smiled it was as if she outshone the sunlight streaming in behind her.

"Lady Emmeline...." Mr. Newbury skirted around his two friends to cross the room to be the first to speak to her. He made a modest but most heartfelt bow.

"Good afternoon, Mr. Newbury. It is quite nice to have you and Sir John join us for tea."

Pauline noticed her friend had omitted mention of her brother.

"It seems the water has just come to a boil. The tea needs to steep for a bit," Mrs. Heffelfinger informed them. "Why don't you lot take a short walk in the garden while you wait?"

"Thank you, Mrs. H, that is an excellent idea." Pauline turned back to her guests and replied, "It will only take a few minutes because the garden is very small." The Conduit Street house had much smaller gardens than those of her family's country house Parklands, where the six of them could roam for hours on end.

"Shall we be on our way, then?" Sir John offered Emmeline his arm.

Mr. Newbury wasted no time and moved quickly to the other side and offered her his arm. "We must make the most of the few minutes we have, mustn't we?" He stepped forward, urging the trio to the double doors that led to the rear gardens.

Emmeline laughed softly.

"Why can we not appear that charming?" Jane whispered, keeping careful watch on the example before them.

"*Charming* is in the eye of the beholder," Lord Epping replied. He offer each his escort and followed his sister.

"You may not consider her charming, but you're her brother." His admission did not make Pauline feel any better. She, and perhaps Jane, needed some help mastering the skill. It could be useful for both of them when they make their Come Out next year.

"Neither one has a true chance with her, you know," Lord Epping confessed to his companions. "Em would not have the least bit of interest in either gentleman."

"Of course not." Jane, who was as new to this Gentleman's Attention as Pauline, remarked. However, they'd both been told, by Emmeline herself, that she wanted to see her choices before making such an important decision. In addition, she wished to enjoy herself.

"How do you know?" Pauline would have thought that if one could attract the attention of a gentleman, a lady could claim his affection. Wasn't that the way it worked?

"Although Em may be close in age to my friends, they hardly hold any interest for her, but the practice is good for them."

"Practice?" Pauline would freely admit there was much to this she did not understand.

"It's the lads' first time in social London. They need a bit of Town Bronze before they get serious about finding a wife." Lord Epping cleared his throat and chuckled. "I have no idea if they even understand that is the end goal. All they see is a pretty face and are drawn to it...*her*."

"Is that what you think?" Pauline wondered if there was something more to attraction or affection than being *handsome* or *pretty*.

"How very sad," Jane echoed a similar sentiment.

"Oh? What is your opinion of young, single persons gathering during the springtime months?"

Despite the scandal of the duel and Martin's broken engagement, Pauline thought the weeks preceding were quite enjoyable. "I should think it is an exciting time. One dresses up and meets new people, attends parties...balls, picnics, and various outings."

"There is that as well, I'll admit." His lordship tightened his arm. Actually, she presumed it was *both* arms, drawing both her hand and Jane's equally as close. "I must confess that I am intrigued by the going-ons I've experienced so far."

"I understand I am not yet Out," said Pauline. "But I have managed to cultivate quite a few new acquaintances in the short time I've been in Town."

"That is very good news because I am a firm believer that one cannot have too many friends." Lord Epping sounded as if he knew he possessed some of what he called Town Bronze.

"Yes, indeed, my lord," Jane agreed.

"*Zounds!* You cannot address me in such a formal manner, Miss Stiles."

"How can I not? You have just now called me *Miss Stiles.*" Jane sounded a bit petulant.

"You cannot convince me that the formality of *my lord* equals the most-proper *Miss.*"

Jane looked about, uncertain of what should be done. "Pauline?"

"Really? You cast about for opinions from your friends to prove you are correct?"

"*Pauline?*" was said with a bit more urgency.

"No. Do not comment, *Pauline,*" Lord Epping cautioned. "I will offer a compromise." Both young ladies gazed at him with rapt attention. "You may address me as *Epping,* and I will address you as *Miss* Jane and *Miss* Pauline, when we are private."

"And why do you suppose we would agree to such familiarity?" Pauline couldn't possibly accept such a thing. Could she?

"Although I have just made the acquaintance of Miss Stiles mere hours ago, my acquaintance with you, Miss Chandler, has been years." By Lord Epping's tone, Pauline might believe he knew something she did not.

Jane audibly gasped. "You never told me that, Pauline!"

"That is not true. It *cannot* be true." For the life of her, Pauline could not remember ever meeting him.

"I think I was just about to go off to Eton and you were no more than five or six."

"Five-years-old?" Pauline exhaled and rolled her eyes. "How do you expect me to remember you at that age?"

"I never thought you would." He chuckled. "Honestly, I don't recall any details myself. I do, however, remember meeting your brother."

"Martin...of course." A second gaze heavenwards was not uncalled for. Could her sibling do no wrong?

"He was much to be admired when I was an impressionable lad," Lord Epping mused. "In any case, although *we* are little-known to one another, our families have been well-acquainted for many years now. I cannot see why the formalities need remain between us. Your family and Miss Stiles' are nearly related as far as I understand."

"Well, we were to be related but all that has changed," Jane corrected, sounding somewhat secretive. She expected he would learn the story, if not from them at some point, then from his mother who would have been told from her mother.

"Should we make allowances for our family's long-standing connection?" Lord Epping put the offer forward.

"I suppose we could...only when we are private, *Epp-ing.*" Pauline tried the more familiar name and glanced nervously at her friend standing on the other side of his lordship.

*Epp-ing...*Jane mouthed, not feeling quite as brave.

"Thank you, Miss *Pauline*, Miss *Jane.*" He smiled.

Hearing Lord Epping—*Epping* speak her Christian name seemed almost more wicked than saying his name aloud. Pauline managed to maintain her composure but Jane giggled.

"Remember, Miss *Jane*, only when we are alone." He cautioned her with a smile. "I have no wish to shock anyone thinking we are over-familiar."

"Of course, sir," Jane managed, doing an excellent job at tamping down her bout of the giggles.

Their group had reached the end of the garden that slowed the two groups, which would bring them soon both to a halt.

"Mind you do not allow Sir John or Mr. Newbury the same familiarity else they will have you calling them *John* and *Hal.*"

That pronouncement made Jane lose what composure she had mustered and she laughed out loud.

"My goodness, Miss Stiles, whatever is the matter?" Emmeline stopped and turned about to gaze at Jane. "Has my brother said something inappropriate? Shame on you, Nicky!"

"I did no such thing, Em," Epping was quick to reply. "Newbury, Sir John!" he barked at his friends. "It's about time you allowed these lovely young ladies to enjoy your company. Although I cannot say why they should do so."

Feeling a bit self-conscious themselves, the two young men stepped away from Emmeline, and whole-heartedly agreed with their friend. Mr. Newbury offered his arm to Jane and it was left to Sir John to escort Pauline.

While Epping was willing to escort his sister, she refused, opting to return to the house unaccompanied.

Only minutes into the journey, because they had not gone far, Mrs. Heffelfinger appeared from the double doors of the dining room at the back of the house. A yodel-like sound came from the chaperone and she waved her arm, to attract their attention.

"Hallo, Mrs. H!" Epping called out, mirroring her motion. "I think she wants us to return," he said to the others.

"I would think so," Emmeline replied.

"We're on our way!" he returned, raising his voice. "We'd best get moving."

"Do let's. I abhor tepid tea." Pauline may have somewhat dragged Sir John toward the house in her haste. The others, although trailing, were not far behind.

"That was quite nice, Mr. Newbury." Jane pulled her hand from the crook of his arm.

"Thank you for your company, Miss Stiles."

Reentering the dining room, Pauline and Sir John were the

first to enter. Jane and Mr. Newbury followed, leaving Emmeline as the last. Epping closed the doors behind them.

The dining room table held several plates of small cakes and biscuits, dotting the center with three chairs placed on either side. A kitchen maid rolled in the tea trolley.

Mrs. Heffelfinger seated herself at the head of the table. It appeared to Pauline that Sir John nor Mr. Newbury, who did not wish to abandon Emmeline's side in the garden, would reclaim their previous positions.

As the first in the room, Mr. Newbury beckoned Emmeline to one side of the table and drew out the center chair, holding it for her.

"Thank you, Mr. Newbury." The earl's daughter happily accepted. Sir John quickly filled the chair on her vacant side.

"I beg you take no offense to my friends' manners, ladies." Epping murmured to Jane and Pauline. He drew the chairs out on the unoccupied side of the table. "If you can endure my company I am quite happy to sit and converse with you."

"Thank you, *Lord* Epping." Pauline took no offense to Sir John's nor Mr. Newbury's preference to sit next to Emmeline. How could they be immune to her beauty?

Sir John leaned forward to collect his cup and saucer. He relaxed back into his chair and hit his knee on the table, sending the china cups and various utensils clattering with an ear-shattering din. The liquid sloshed in its containers, sending some dangerously close to overflowing its confines.

"I beg your pardon!" Sir John spat out in shock.

"Of course you do, I imagine you did not do so intentionally." Pauline tried to calm her guest.

"No—no, of course not."

"*Lord* Epping," Jane began, filling the silence. "Tell us, have you been in Town long?"

"Only arrived last week," he replied. "I look forward to all the gatherings. It is a shame we can't attend any grand parties."

"We haven't been invited to any grand parties," Jane replied, rather glumly.

"Gracious no!" Mrs. Heffelfinger snapped. "I should think not!"

"The Countess of Chesney puts on a Sunday party that is very nice." Mr. Newbury informed them.

"Oh?" Remarked Jane and Pauline with interest.

"She does a great service to young persons, gives us a chance to brush up our etiquette and such. I'm certain it is not difficult to procure an invitation."

"Countess of Chesney?" With the tilt of her head, Jane took some time to think before she spoke. "I think I may be related to her."

"What? Is she a *cousin* of yours too?" Pauline knew of Jane's extensive family tree while the others did not. It was a distinct possibility.

"Seems as if everyone is, one way or another. I would not be so quick as to deny it," Jane stated a bit meekly. "If we are not related then she may be a friend of my mother's. I'm sure it would not hurt to make inquiries."

SEVEN

EMMELINE ATTENDED LORD AND Lady Miltham's party that evening with her mother, who presently conversed with the hostess, while Mrs. Peckover stood in the chaperone's corner and peered at her charge.

"It is very good to see you again, Lady Emmeline." Miss Hester Enfield was the first to approach that evening. Em recognized the strained expression of isolation and abandonment and the relief upon finally landing upon a familiar face.

"And you, Miss Enfield." Em sensed the unease in her companion and tried to comfort her by saying, "Thank you for keeping me company. I was beginning to feel quite alone."

"Nonsense." Hester's quick smile and sudden sigh told Em that she had distracted her friend, if only momentarily. "Lady Em...." She took a second, longer look, carefully studying Em's gown. "How well you look and you have managed to turn a white gown into something truly magnificent. The trim around your neck and arms absolutely shimmers."

"Thank you for noticing. It is rather nice, isn't it?" Em glanced at her arms, admiring the golden glimmer from the sleeves. "I found this trim while shopping this morning and my chaperone Mrs. Peckover was kind enough to alter my gown in time for this evening's party."

Hester looked very fine, however...there was an odd expression...or something in her demeanor that told of some discomfort.

"Gracious, Hester, whatever is it?" Em could not keep from thinking all was not right with her.

She caught her lower lip between her teeth and with a distressed look, wrung her hands. "I'm afraid I have not made a very good impression on Lord Charles Foster during our last set."

Em had yet to have the pleasure of meeting his lordship and expected it would only be a matter of time before she did but could not warrant that her companion should fret so. "Why ever not? Did he not notice your pretty eyes? Your charming smile?" Hester was every bit as beautiful as any of the young ladies in attendance.

"I was nervous, of course, and he was quite handsome." Hester glanced at Em, seeming quite shy.

"You, Hester, have quite a few good qualities besides appearance. If success was merely based on being *handsome*, everyone in Town would claim themselves a champion."

"But he was *very* handsome."

"Very well." Em chuckled. "I will take your word that Lord Charles is more handsome than any of the other gentlemen in attendance. Why should that make you nervous?"

"He looked at me." She flushed.

"I believe he is supposed to look at you. That is how you will entrance him...with your beauty."

"He made me feel so nervous." Her breaths were controlled and labored as Hester struggled to keep herself calm.

"Did he speak to you? Did you speak to him?" Em found Hester Enfield quite amusing.

"Yes, he said, 'How do you do?' to me."

"And you replied in kind, of course."

"Yes, I did." The suffusion of pink deepened in her cheeks. Hester was the nicest of females. If she would only behave in the same manner with men as she did with Em...she would not have a problem at all.

"Hester...you are your own worst enemy." Miss Enfield's nerves would be the end of her! "You are perfectly lovely and have nothing to worry about."

Two young ladies approached. Lady Amelia, known to Em and Hester, had met at a party more than a week ago. The raven-haired beauty would turn any man's head. The second, they would need an introduction....

"Lady Emmeline, Miss Enfield," Lady Amelia greeted them. "May I introduce my new acquaintance?"

"I would be delighted," Em replied. Hester, who managed to regain her composure, smiled at the newcomers and agreed with a nod.

"Lady Emmeline, Miss Enfield, may I present Miss Danvers?"

"How do you do?" Miss Danvers performed a shallow but respectful curtsy. Dressed in the same sort of white gown as every other young lady in attendance, she was here for her first Season.

"How do you do, Miss Danvers?" Hester and Em chorused.

"Do tell us something of yourself." The ever-curious Hester was doing her utmost to draw information out of the newcomer. It seemed that Miss Danvers had been in Town for quite some time and had made the acquaintance of many others in Town.

"Lady Emmeline?" The hostess approached their group. "I

have been asked by a particular gentleman to make him known to you," she whispered.

How nice. Em's first *requested* introduction. She turned to her friends to excuse herself and followed Lady Miltham. How Em had waited, dreamed of this moment. It seemed as if it might never arrive. She drew in a breath and swung her gaze to the tall, well-dressed young man standing next to the hostess.

"Lord Hoswell, may I introduce you to Lady Emmeline Cordia-Darling?"

"How do you do, Lady Emmeline?" Lord Hoswell did not disappoint. He was the type of gentleman Em had expected to see in London. Tall, lean, and very handsome. If all the gentlemen were of this caliber it would make choosing among them difficult if one were to judge them by their appearance. No one knew better than she that one's exterior did not always reflect one's true self.

Em knew what was expected of her and she would ultimately comply—there would be no disappointing her family. Until then, she wished to enjoy herself.

"How do you do, Lord Hoswell?" She graced him with a polite smile and glanced shyly away. She couldn't help but feel a little timid at such direct attention paid to her.

"I must confess I saw you standing across the room and I knew at once I must beg an introduction from our hostess."

"You are kind to say so." Em, in a graceful, fluid motion, brought her hands together then extended her gloved hand to touch the lower edge of her puffed sleeve to bring attention to her arm.

Lord Hoswell watched the gesture with quiet interest and cleared his throat. "Lady Miltham tells me you have just arrived and this is your first Season."

"It is. I have not made many acquaintances." And his lordship was the first gentleman for her consideration. Em wasn't about to tell him that bit, and it was her secret that no matter how wealthy, how charming, or how handsome—she was not to be tempted by such shallow qualities. She gazed at him, renewing her smile.

"I would like to claim the next country dance, if I may."

"Thank you, my lord." Em curtsied again.

"I look forward to our next meeting." He bowed over her hand then turned to the hostess. "Thank you, Lady Miltham for the honor of the introduction."

"My pleasure, Lord Hoswell." Lady Miltham inclined her head then turned to wink at Emmeline.

Crossing the room to where her group stood, she heard Miss Danvers whisper to Lady Amelia and Miss Enfield, "That was *Joshua*...Lord Hoswell."

"I have heard that he might be the catch of the Season," Miss Enfield whispered to Lady Amelia and Miss Danvers.

"Really?" Amelia, who arrived in Town approximately the same time Em had, did not know of Lord Hoswell...until now. She did not appear envious of Em, merely curious.

"He looks well enough but I think I would need to become better acquainted to make that decision." Em thought it was not best to make a judgement based on one's first impression. "I will have more to base an opinion after we have shared a dance." She blinked and uttered wistfully, "It will be my very first."

"I cannot believe you have not been asked to dance before now. You must be this Season's *Incomparable*."

"Amelia!" Em scolded her friend while her skirts swirled, sending sparkles of light skimming along the surface of the floor. Apparently, Mrs. Peckover had used the golden trim along the hemline of the dress as well. "Please, you put me to the blush!"

Waiting for her brother's return home was agonizing. Jane sat on the sofa in the sitting room of Grayson House and snipped the thread after pulling her needle through her work for the final time. "I'm sure I'm only feeling sorry for myself, Mrs. H, but I feel so alone." She set the small scissors in the sewing box and reached for her *étui*.

"And how are you alone if I am sitting here next to you?" The elder lady did not look up from her knitting.

"Oh, Auntie! I did not mean to say you are not here or that you do not matter." Jane laid her hand on her aunt's arm to reassure her. "Don't be silly."

"I didn't know what you were thinking...being alone and all." Mrs. Heffelfinger chuckled.

"Are you not lonely, with just the two of us here?" Jane thought their isolation was very sad.

"You are young and I think when one is young one craves other young people around them...not an old woman like me."

"Do not say such things, Auntie. You are not old."

"It's not a bad thing. You cannot help being young. I was young once. I understand." She nodded her head. "If Sir Christopher were here, he'd be company enough for you, I warrant."

"I know he would be." Jane could feel her throat constrict. Soon her eyes would fill with tears and then she would become a watering pot.

"I am sure there are a few days more until he returns home. Why do we not plan something for ourselves?"

"Such as?"

"After our shopping with the Chandlers and their friends, I would say you've made a new friend, Lady Emmeline."

"I suppose I have." There was nothing sad about that.

"What if we arranged a card party? Three young ladies and three older women, that would make six. We could manage, couldn't we?"

"But eight would be better." Jane thought two tables of four would make for a more comfortable party.

"Certainly." Mrs. Heffelfinger lowered her needles, shifting her attention from her knitting to her niece. "Well...there is someone we could send an invitation to. Someone we've just met who is loosely related and may also welcome a pleasant diversion."

Jane gasped, recalling their most recent visitors. "Lady Frances and her mother or her chaperone?"

"Lady Frances may not be popular with the Society crowd at the moment because of the near scandal but we could make her feel a bit more welcome in this house."

"That is a wonderful idea, Aunt." Jane could not have thought of a better prospect, her aunt was so clever. "And very thoughtful, as well."

"I don't see how that could hurt any if we were to include her." Mrs. Heffelfinger pulled at her ball of yarn.

"I'll write the invitations at once and we can send them out in the morning." Jane put away her sewing basket, left, then returned with ink, quill, and paper, settling near the small table. "For what day should we plan this, Auntie?"

"Not tomorrow...what about the day after?" Mrs. Heffelfinger continued her knitting.

"Thursday? Very well. That will give us time for all the guests to make plans and we can tell Cook to bake those small cakes of hers." How Kit loved those cakes. It was a shame he could not be here to enjoy them. "It should be plenty of time to prepare, I should think."

"Cook will want to know if there'll be six extra mouths to feed for an afternoon's entertainment." Mrs. Heffelfinger nodded. "She won't thank you for keeping this from her longer than you need."

"What do you think about inviting Lord Epping, Mr. Newbury, and Sir John?" Jane imagined they would be great fun, but would it be appropriate?

"They may enjoy themselves but I can assure you they will not have their minds on card games."

"No?"

"No. I do not think so." Mrs. Heffelfinger nodded, quite certain. "Best leave them out. Having a Ladies Only afternoon will serve for the present."

"Very well, Auntie." Jane focused on the paper before her and took her time to pen the invitations, for she would only need three.

AT THE MILTHAM HOUSE PARTY, IT ONLY TOOK LORD HOSWELL'S interest in Emmeline for the remainder of the eligible males in attendance to come around for an introduction...or so it appeared to Em. She had a partner for every dance, all of whom she had met just that evening. By association, Em's small group with whom she'd kept company, experienced nearly the very same success with the gentlemen guests.

After their country dance, Lord Hoswell returned Em to the safety of her group. It took her a few minutes to recover from the excitement of spending time with him. Now she understood why Lady Miltham was so pleased to make introductions.

"What are your thoughts about Lord Hoswell?" Hester inquired softly, only for Em's ears.

"I must admit he is more than merely a handsome face." Why was it she could not stop smiling? It wasn't just talking about him. Em could not stop thinking about him. "I find him quite charming."

"Will you see him again?"

"Tomorrow." Em tried to suppress her smile. "He is to take me for a drive in the Park." She did not wish to appear as if she was smitten. It was this very type of behavior she could not abide in others. Em never wanted to commit oneself to any one gentleman...she wished to pick and choose among those around her.... However, when one only had a single suitor...that was, if she could call Lord Hoswell a suitor. She did not know if he was, as of yet. Only time would tell.

"His lordship asked me the strangest questions. He wanted to know if I objected to receiving flowers from him." Em thought that one of the loveliest gestures a young lady could receive was a posey or two from an admirer.

"Why should you object?" Hester must have thought the notion was equally as odd. "I would adore them above all things."

Em could admit to herself that his offering might be lonely as the only bouquet she received in her family's home but it would be welcome all the same.

"Have you heard about the duel?" Amelia pulled Em to one side and whispered.

"A duel? Is his lordship involved?" The words took her breath away...to think...she'd only just met him and now...if he were to perish in a duel!

"No, not Lord Hoswell." Amelia shook her head. "It seems

Lord Keene took great offense to Sir Jeremy Hunt's waistcoat," Amelia told her at once.

"A waistcoat?" Em could not have heard correctly. "There is to be a duel over a waistcoat?" Over a garment? Weren't duels supposed to be over ladies? Quarreling over her affections? Protecting her honor? "What sort of nonsense is—"

"I thought Sir Jeremy looked rather splendid." Amelia must have appeared rather like a mooncalf in contemplating the gentleman. Em had the notion it was not the waistcoat that attracted her friend to the baronet.

Miss Danvers, escorted by Mr. Pelham, rejoined their group after the completion of the most recent set. He thanked her kindly for the dance and left.

"Miss Danvers," Amelia addressed her immediately upon her arrival. "Did you not drive to the Park with Lord Hoswell?"

"No, I did not," she said in a most curt and stern attitude.

"Oh, I thought you...." Amelia gazed upon her and declared, "I must have been mistaken."

"I expect Mr. Pelham to call tomorrow morning."

"I am certain he will," Amelia agreed.

"I find him quite agreeable." Miss Danvers' smile appeared to be a bit forced, tight. She wondered who Miss Danvers was trying to convince...Amelia or herself.

Miss Enfield, was the last of their group to return a few moments later, escorted by Mr. Gilbert.

"And you, Hester?" Em, turned to her friend. "What did you think of Mr. Gilbert?"

"I do not think he wished to attend tonight," she stated quite frankly. "He was not in mind to enjoy the dance, nor, I'm afraid, were his feet. I had to take care my new slippers were not trod upon."

"How could he not enjoy himself? That cannot be right?" Em thought there could not be a more splendid party. The lights, the decor, the people...all were quite exciting and exceptional.

"All he could do was ramble on about some duel." Hester sounded quite bored of the topic.

"Not the duel over a waistcoat?" It was easily the most ridiculous thing Em had heard in her entire life.

"No. This was something quite serious." Apparently Hester was not bored as much as exasperated. "It's just...I do not wish to hear another word about it."

"Do not tell me—" Em could not help but poke fun at her misfortune. "They faced one-another over a pair of overly-large, baggy pair of breeches?"

"*Em-mel-ine!*" The three others shrieked, covering their mouths, both outraged and amused at the mention of male unmentionables.

"No." Hester fought to catch her breath. "They dueled over a lady's honor."

"There's a *second* duel?" Miss Danvers, who had been the messenger of the first, became quite alarmed. Had she thought that perhaps Mr. Gilbert's fears were not as unfounded as she believed?

"No, this one's already finished, a few days ago." Hester shook her head. "Mr. Gilbert thinks he will be somehow embroiled in a questionable situation and forced to face some other gentleman on the *field of honor*."

"I find that unlikely." Em narrowed her eyes, wondering if this Gilbert-*person* could be believed.

"Exactly." Hester leaned near to whisper, "The man is a quiz."

That was not a very nice thing to say. Em did not think he

could have been as bad as that, and it was not like Hester to be so judgmental.

"He had some absurd notion that if Sir Christopher were here, there would be some controversy fabricated between them." The tone of Hester's voice was not one of retelling of an amusing story.

"*Sir Christopher*?" Amelia repeated. "Do you mean Sir Christopher Glory?"

"The very one."

Surely he is not the same *Sir Christopher* as Miss Stiles' brother? This surprised Em more than news of either duel.

"I have heard his name spoken several times this evening." Amelia glanced about as if looking for him. "Have you seen him? Where is he?"

"It seems he had not been seen since the duel." Hester busied herself by straightening the fingers of her glove. "Apparently Lord Linwood uttered some disparaging words about Sir Christoper Glory's sister, Miss Victoria Abbott."

This must have been Miss Stiles' much mentioned sister *Victoria,* whom she and Pauline Chandler had discussed the other night. Em's interest in Lord Hoswell and Lord Charles Foster, who had been mentioned earlier that evening, began to ebb in favor of learning more of Sir Christopher.

"Do you think he's left the country?" Amelia gave up her search for the baronet.

"It seems unlikely since Lord Linwood was not harmed."

"That is very curious." Except Em knew, Sir Christopher had gone to Bath, and she was not about to say how she had come upon this information. Not until she learned why Miss Stiles and Miss Chandler did not tell her of his involvement in the duel earlier.

eight

THE NEXT MORNING EMMELINE awoke thinking of last night's wonderful party. She would soon begin her toilette, prepare for her calls but first she would sip on her chocolate and peruse the invitations her mother had left for her.

For the most part Lady Kennington chose which parties to consider and left the final decision to Em. She usually went along with whatever her mother decided, thinking her parent, most probably, knew best.

Em had heard such wonderful gossip, including the news about Miss Stiles' brother Sir Christopher during the party. After further consideration she realized that Miss Stiles had not said a word when they met the other night because of the potential scandal. It would have been most improper to announce that one's brother had fought in a duel that morning upon making someone's acquaintance.

Flipping past the first few invitations, Em noticed a handwritten card from Jane Stiles inviting Em and her mother to a small card party. Lifting the card, she read it with interest. It would be a select number attending, as there was the other night, with Jane's aunt, and surely the Chandler ladies. Emmeline gladly accepted because currying favor with Miss Stiles would make meeting Sir Christopher all the more easy.

ARRIVING IN BATH, SIR CHRISTOPHER GLORY, WITH HIS WALKING stick in hand, exited the traveling coach before it had rolled to a full stop in front of their Laura Place destination.

"Do be careful, Christopher!" his mother called out a needless caution. "The vehicle is still in motion!"

Remaining another minute longer in the company of the two females, in particular his sister Victoria, would have been unbearable for him. How she could maintain her hard stare, most probably wishing him dead if not to the confines of hell, for both legs of their journey, Christopher did not know.

"See to the ladies, will you?" he instructed the footman, riding next to the driver in the box. Christopher trotted up the stairs and applied the door knocker, then brushed his coat with the back of his gloved hands.

The door opened and the butler intoned, "We have been expecting you, Sir Christopher," and allowed him entrance into the townhouse.

Christopher, who just pulled off his gloves, dropped them in his hat, and handed them, along with his walking stick, to the butler before removing his traveling coat.

"Briggs, at your service, sir," the servant informed the visitor, taking the proffered outer raiment.

"Thank you, Briggs." Turning about to take in his surroundings, Christopher felt the buzz of the household when he entered.

"Sir Christopher!" His hostess approached wearing a lovely day dress and a lace cap.

"Lady Belton, it is very good to see you again." He bowed over her hand. Even though it had been some years since their last meeting, he recognized her at once. "On behalf of my family, I must thank you for your gracious offer."

"I am delighted to have company...especially family, Sir Christopher," Lady Belton replied. "I have been forever attempting to lure your mother, one of my dearest friends, to Bath for a respite. Eh...those years she was not married, of course."

"There is no need to go on." Christopher held up his hand. It was daunting enough to keep track of his mother's children, husbands, and marriages, he would never expect someone outside the family to do so. "I understand completely."

"Where is she?" Lady Belton glanced around his person. "And what of Miss Abbott?"

"It will be only moments before they join us," he reassured their hostess. "It was most gracious of you to accept Victoria. I realize your invitation had not originally included her."

"Oh, it is nothing, I can assure you!" Lady Belton continued, "It will be a delight to count her among our company."

"As I have already written, there has been some *unpleasant-ness* in Town and—"

"There is no need to explain. I am certain I will learn all from your mother in due time." She called to the butler, "Briggs, have a tea tray sent to the front parlor and see that the special nuncheon is set out."

"Very well, my lady." Briggs bowed and stepped from their sight.

"Will I not be joining you ladies?" Christopher felt some-what abandoned. Was he to be confined to the outer edges of the house? Isolated from the two older ladies' reunion and inclusive feminine congregation? The separation did not truly offend him, but he did not think it quite hospitable. On second thought, it was not such a horrid notion.

"All will be revealed after you've freshened up from your travels."

"Your behavior is quite cryptic, ma'am." Christopher did not know what to think. For a gentleman who was used to self-managing and knowing the comings and goings around him, he found Lady Belton's machinations a bit disconcerting.

"Yes, yes. Isn't it fun?" she said with a swell of laughter. "You will be so delighted! I promise you."

By this time Lady Yardley and Victoria had made their way from the coach, up the front steps, and into the foyer.

"There you are!" Lady Belton, approaching her friend and once sister-in-law with outstretched arms for a warm welcome.

"How good it is to see you again, Tilly." Lady Yardley pressed her cheeks against her friend's. She motioned behind her. "You recall meeting my eldest daughter Victoria."

"Oh, yes." Lady Belton turned to the younger female.

"How do you do, my lady?" Victoria curtsied.

"But it has been many years, and look how you have grown... so very lovely. You will turn many heads, and perhaps break a few hearts, in this fair city." Lady Belton nodded in approval. "We shall visit the Pump Room, take the waters, and we must add your name to the subscription books so the Master of Cere-monies will pay us a call." She gave Victoria a second, more searching inspection. "Perhaps only the Upper Rooms, I think. We will make quite the impression with Sir Christopher in our company."

"I hate to disappoint you, my lady, I must inform you that it is not my intent to remain in Bath for long."

"What's that you say, sir?" It did not sound as if Lady Belton cared for Christopher's plans.

"I thank you, ma'am, for allowing Lady Yardley and my sister Victoria to share your house for the summer but I must return to London immediately."

"You don't mean you are to leave us?"

"First thing in the morning, ma'am."

"That is not to be borne." Lady Belton recoiled and took hold of Lady Yardley's forearm for support.

"It must be, I'm afraid." Christopher shrugged, helpless to accede to her wishes. He had responsibilities, more than to these females. Jane waited in Town for him.

"Grace, my dear, do tell your son he cannot deny us his company."

"I'm afraid he is quite above the age of doing as his mother says." Lady Yardley glanced at her son and smiled. Christopher knew how much his mother adored him.

"Well, we shall see if I cannot change your mind, eh?" Lady Belton waited until the front door closed before she continued. "I've sent for tea and by the time you've seen your room and freshened up a bit, we'll have a sit-down and catch-up. Some of us need to get reacquainted. It has been far too long." She gave Christopher a wink.

What, he wondered, was that about?

CHRISTOPHER RETURNED TO THE PARLOR TO FIND LADY BELTON alone. She paced the length of the room, waiting for him. There was something more affecting her than the excitement of her new visitors.

"Finally, you are here." Her ladyship welcomed Christopher

and laced her arm through his and led him out of the parlor and farther down the corridor. "I have a little surprise for you."

"For me?" Christopher could not help but feel a bit suspicious regarding his hostess' behavior. "This journey was to be a reunion for you and Lady Yardley."

"It will be, never fear. But there has been another unexpected occurrence, something for which I have wished—hoped for a very long time." She must have sensed his hesitance and comforted him with, "Now, have no fear. All will be well, you shall see."

"I cannot imagine what you have in mind, Lady Belton." Christopher would humor her and hopefully this surprise of hers would not be too much of a shock.

They turned the corner into what he understood to be the library, but sitting at a large table was—

"Good God, *Albee*!"

"*Kit*! You rascal, you!" Albert Winslow stood from a chair and in three long strides, crossed the room and greeted him with a great hug.

Christopher clapped his longtime friend on the back. "It is so very good to see you." They took a step back from one another to have a second look, making certain his eyes had not deceived him. "Really good to see you."

"I'm going to send in a nuncheon for you gentlemen—" Lady Belton interrupted the two longtime friends. "And you two can have a nice undisturbed visit."

"Thank you, Aunt Tilly."

"I am so happy that I have had a hand in bringing you together. You take your time and enjoy yourselves." Lady Belton left, closing the door behind her.

"Shall we have a seat?" Albee motioned to the chairs at the table where he first sat.

"Delighted." Christopher drew the hard-backed chair from the table. "It's been an age. You look good." Although dressed neatly, Albee was not one to adopt any current fashion. He lived on his country estate, somewhat of a recluse, since their Eton years. His friend stood a bit taller, his hair was a bit darker, his frame a bit leaner. Albee had grown, looking more like a man than the boy Christopher remembered.

Albert Winslow may have appeared near the same to his friend, except *inside,* he was not exactly the same. Kit hadn't married, lost a wife and a newborn son. Those things had probably aged Albert beyond his years. He may not have looked it, but he certainly felt it.

"What are you doing here?"

"I decided it was time I came back. Aunt Tilly has been after me to come visit her since—since—right after I lost Elizabeth."

"I'm sorry for that. I wish there was something I could have done for you."

"There wasn't anything anyone could have done." Albert had cried, he'd mourned, and after some time had passed he'd stopped feeling anything. The only part that hadn't died was the part that breathed. How he had stayed alive, he didn't know.

"How long has it been?" Kit asked.

"Two years, almost three now. Too long. I should have never shut myself away." Albert felt bad that he'd lost contact with his friend. After the loss of his family he'd cut himself off from the outside world, feeling he had no reason to continue.

This year Aunt Tilly had written to him. She did so just after the start of every year, inviting him to spend the spring and summer with her in Bath. He had planned to write to decline and thank her for her offer as he always had. This year was different.

Was it the wording of her invitation? The fact that she

missed his company? Perhaps it was the way she explained to him that if he continued on this path he would be destined to lead a life wasted and that was not to be tolerated.

He took her at her word and it was enough for him to accept. He'd been selfish and neglectful. Aunt Tilly, Lady Belton, was his favorite aunt and he didn't want her to be alone and then it occurred to him that he shouldn't be alone either. It was then he realized his life had to change.

Albert would never stop loving Elizabeth and their babe, but they were gone. He would never forget them, but he had to make himself go on.

He would keep his aunt company in Bath. He could attend a party or two, make new acquaintances. Perhaps dance once again. He might even find cause to smile. If he had made this much of an effort in almost three years, think how far he could progress in ten.

"How is your family?" Albert knew that was a question that might take a great deal of time to answer.

With a sigh, Kit brought a thoughtful hand to his jaw. "Must I go through the lot from the beginning?"

"Perhaps we will take them a bit at a time." Albert chuckled. "Is your mother still married?"

"Not presently and she's been widowed for the tenth time."

"*Ten*! Gad!" Albert nearly reeled back. "The last I heard she was Lady Worsham."

"She is now Lady Yardley Grayson." Kit then clarified, "Youngest son of the Duke of Dolan."

"What became of Lord Worsham?" Albert was almost afraid to hear.

"Apoplexy." Kit shook his head at delivering the bad news.

"And Lord Yardley?"

"His was another untimely demise. Unexpected and, thankfully, relatively quick—you know how it is for her." Kit did not need to explain. "Since Grayson, she has remained unattached. Mama marries her admirers, advances her position, acquires wealth—all by following her heart. I cannot think how devastating it could be in a world where women quite frequently die in childbirth. It has been the opposite with her. She bears children and mourns their fathers' passing."

"Men usually beget heirs and father children only to lose their wife in childbirth." As Albert, himself, had.

After knocking, three footmen entered carrying a bottle of claret, bread, and a board of cold meats and cheeses which were set on the table before them.

"Lady Bolton was very thoughtful to provide us with a meal and some privacy." Kit sounded grateful for their situation. He glanced up as he helped himself to the bread. "I have not travelled to Bath alone. Did your aunt not tell you?"

"No, she did not. Perhaps you will fill me in." Albert reached for the cheese, thankful they had such a splendid repast to help them become reacquainted and pass the time.

"I'm afraid it is a long story." Kit unfastened the buttons of his coat and removed the garment before sitting, making himself more comfortable.

"We have nothing but time." Albert froze, astonished at the sight before him. Not quite believing his eyes, he blinked. "Is that what the well-dressed gentlemen are wearing in Town nowadays?"

"What is it? The cut of my trousers? The cravat? The jacket?" Kit glanced downward at his apparel while performing a slow circle.

"The pattern of your waistcoat is most...distracting. I am trying to be as kind as I can so as to not to hurt your feelings, my friend."

"You wound me. I found this exceptional tailor when I arrived in Town and had him conjure up several of these creations. I thought it rather smart." Kit must have honestly *liked* the print. "I thought I might set the next trend, give Brummell some competition...he is not the only one who can lead fashion."

Albert took a second look and considered that this was one trend that should not be followed. The *garment,* for one had to call it that, was horrid—garish, overly saturated with too many colors for his taste, and to state it plainly, it was ugly. Dare he say it...offensive?

"Come now, Kit. Have a seat and do catch me up with your family." Albert placed a bit of meat and cheese on his plate and prepared himself for the lengthy discourse to follow.

Kit settled on the opposite side of the food-laden table and made himself comfortable. Thank goodness Albert could only see his friend above the waist and most of the time, his white shirtsleeves blocked the view of the unattractive pattern that lay behind.

"Very well. My elder brothers, Harry, Sam, and Will have all reached their majority and currently run their fathers' estates. Quite successfully, I might add, and contribute quite generously, to the maintenance of our large, extended family."

Financial aid to a family the size of Lady Yardley's could not be more welcomed. Albert did not mean to imply anything untoward when it came to the running of her life and that of her children. The task must have been a chore unto itself. Kit was the fourth son and had only just reached his majority recently.

"John, Robert, William, and his brother Frederick currently attend Eton. Your cousins Stephen and Peter Beeson, seven and six, will soon be heading for that academic establishment."

"My mother's two subsequent marriages after your Uncle

Beeson produced four more sons, who are all currently below the age of five."

Good God!

"Then there are my two sisters, Jane and Victoria."

"Ah, yes. The only two females. I do recall them." Albert chewed slowly, not wishing to hurry his friend.

"I expect we will have quite a lengthy discussion there, I'm afraid. They.... Victoria...has been more trouble to me than all of my brothers combined." Kit became rather sober and straightened in his chair with the realization. "We will spend one evening in their company and you will see how those women will do their utmost to wind you about until they achieve their objectives." He lifted his glass and took a deep drink. "If you know what one female can do, can you imagine three?"

It occurred to Albert.... "Aunt Tilly has already planned our outings for the remainder of the week." He could well-imagine their plans might change with the arrival of the new visitors.

"May I remind you Lady Yardley has a large number of friends she has not seen in a very long while. And if she should need an escort, you will be the handy male. Worse yet, there is my sister Victoria...."

"Little innocent Vic?"

"She is no longer *little* and I cannot vouch for her *innocence.* If she should manage to work her way around you...." Kit shook his head. "My friend Martin has just escaped her neat parson's mousetrap."

"How can you say such a thing? She's your sister."

"And two days hence I found myself dueling to uphold her reputation. One, I daresay, I am not wholly certain is worthy. My sister is not my mother." Kit swallowed the last of his claret. "I leave for Town in the morning." He glanced over his shoulder at the door and lowered his volume. "If you had any sense, you'd abandon Bath and join me in London."

"I don't know if I'm ready to throw myself into that Lion's Den."

"I warn you, if you remain you may find yourself in greater danger."

"What do you mean?"

"Three women in one house with you as the only escort. Nothing but trouble can come of that." Kit reached for the decanter and refilled his glass. "I've just relocated two family members from Grayson House to Bath. All who remain at the Bruton Street house are an elderly aunt who acts as chaperone for Jane, who is not yet Out, and me. The house is large and you may choose to lose yourself there if you wish...in safety, I might add."

Kit drank deep from his glass again while Albert considered his offer.

THREE HOURS LATER, EMMELINE, NOW COIFFED AND DRESSED, descended the staircase of Kennington House more bleary-eyed than normal to find her mother surrounded by floral arrangements. Em blinked, wondering if she was still asleep. It looked to her as if a flower shop, or three, had set up in her foyer.

"Mama?" After only her morning chocolate for sustenance, Em knew she was not fully awake. "What is this—*are* all these?"

"All *these*, my dear, are from your admirers." Lady Kennington smiled wide, quite pleased with the jungle of floral tributes surrounding her.

There were so many! Em assumed there might have been a

few because she had danced every dance but not enough to warrant this number.

"The gentlemen with whom you danced last night, I expect." Lady Kennington went from one floral arrangement to the next, delighting in the beauty of each. "And those you met and to whom you denied the pleasure." She nodded in comprehension. "They hope to make some favorable impression and I would not put it past them to call this morning."

Em's head was spinning. Was it because her stomach was empty? How was it that her presence had gone virtually unnoticed for her first two weeks in Town, but after attending the party last night, she was now receiving such a plethora of flowers?

"There you are!" Mrs. Peckover entered from the corridor. "I would imagine there will be gentlemen callers falling all over themselves this day. You'd best have breakfast, Lady Emmeline, and prepare yourself."

"How many callers?" Em wondered.

"As many as there are flowers around you," her chaperone replied, taking hold of her arm to lead her away. Em turned her head to stare at them over her shoulder as they moved down the corridor to the breakfast room.

Mrs. Peckover could not have meant that. Em understood morning calls were brief, sedate, and polite visits. To accommodate that number of visitors would prove to be chaos.

"Do keep an eye on the time, Mrs. Peckover, will you?" Lady Kennington gave the gentle reminder. "Do not forget that Em is to accompany Lord Hoswell to the Park at the fashionable hour."

Of course, he was the only gentleman who held any true interest for Em. No matter how many others were to call this morning.

nine

HAMPSTEAD HEATH

"SEVEN! EIGHT! NINE! TEN!"

Lord Keene and Sir Jeremy Hunt stopped when the count ended and turned to face one another. The morning was cool, the visibility excellent. There was no mist to inhibit the participants' sight.

Sir Jeremy, holding his pistol, barrel pointed toward the sky, drew back his jacket, displaying his garish blue-green-yellow monstrosity of a waistcoat...or so his lordship thought.

"Gad! Need you taunt me further?" Lord Keene shouted across the way. "As if I needed more of a reason to shoot you! If I am lucky my shot will hit you so you'll bleed through that damned abomination!"

"You, Keene, hold such outdated aesthetics that do not allow you to move beyond lace cuffs!" Sir Jeremy delivered the low-key insult to his opponent amongst the chuckles of the onlooking crowd who had gathered to enjoy the morning's entertainment.

"Young jackanapes! You will never learn to spot a decent fashionable trend," Lord Keene slung back.

"I would hate to see an end to our friendship for you are the best drinking mate," Sir Jeremy confessed. Could the value of sitting down with an amiable chum over a glass of canary outweigh their disagreement? One must not take that quality of association lightly.

"If that is so, then I ask that you take pity upon me and refrain from wearing such garments when in my company." It was his lordship's suggestion towards a satisfactory compromise.

There was a collective holding of breaths. Would this disagreement resolve? Surely, death could not be the answer to this fashion *faux pas*. Tension held the on-lookers glued to the pair as the resolution to this dramatic vignette may have come into sight.

Sir Jeremy pursed his lips while considering the proposition. "I suppose that is a reasonable request." Sir Jeremy nodded his head thoughtfully. "Very well, Keene."

The relief that one friend would not kill the other overtook the small gathering. Shouts of support, how good sense had prevailed, the general agreement for the outcome circulated. Friend would not injure friend this day.

Lord Keene smiled, pleased with their resolution. Returning a good-natured grin, Sir Jeremy extended his arm upward and fired his pistol overhead. The sound of his discharging pistol was immediately followed by the unexpected solid crack of wood.

The once affable aspects of the two men facing one another and the standing crowd all glanced about confused by the disturbance. The free-falling branch from above was followed by a resounding *THUNK*. A large limb had landed on a curricle, that stood to one side, sending a team of horses bolting forward into a group of men standing off the dueling field to the horror and cries of the onlookers.

A man cried out, falling to the ground. He grasped his right thigh and rolled about in pain.

"Good God, Hackett!" Lord Keene shouted. Both he and Sir Jeremy ran toward their acquaintance.

"Stand aside! Stand aside!" Mr. Brathwaite pushed through the gathering crowd to get at the fallen man. Despite the point that he was not involved in the duel, the surgeon would see to his care. "Let me see the injured man. It is fortunate for you, lad, that I am here."

It pleased Christopher that he had successfully convinced Albee to accompany him to Town. His friend may not have realized just yet how fortunate his actions would prove.

"Is there nothing I can do to make you stay?" Lady Belton must have realized the futility of her pleas. Lady Yardley and Victoria Abbott stood with her in the foyer.

"We were hoping you would escort us to the Upper Assembly Rooms...accompany us to the Pump Rooms, at least."

"I'm afraid that is quite impossible, ma'am. I have left my young sister Jane in the care of her chaperone Mrs. Heffelfinger and I dare not make my absence any longer than need be."

"I cannot believe you are to leave us, Albert!" Lady Belton turned to her nephew.

Christopher approached his mother to buss her cheeks. "Farewell, dear Mama."

"Aunt, I thank you for your hospitality." Albee bowed over Lady Belton's hand.

"All this time it took to get you here and you leave so soon!" she cried out.

"There will be another time, I am sure, dear aunt." Albee nodded to the other ladies. "A pleasure to make your acquaintance, Lady Yardley, Miss Abbott."

The stable lad arrived with the two horses and the coach with their luggage would soon follow.

"Lady Belton, I have a request to make of you." Christopher took the reins of his horse.

"What would that be, Sir Christopher? What could this old woman possibly do for you?"

"I beg you, Lady Belton, you will not allow gentlemen to make love to my dear Mama."

Lady Yardley gasped and giggled. "Christopher!"

"And an elopement, Lady Belton, under any circumstances, is absolutely forbidden. I will be quite cross."

"Christopher—*really!*" Lady Yardley scolded.

"Do remember if you are to tumble into love while I am away, Mama, you know my requirements for your next—"

"Christopher!" Lady Yardley cried out and giggled in embarrassment. "You are *impossible!* I am *not* looking for a husband."

"You never are, dear ma'am. However, it always seems to happen. You have been unattached for these last two years. I cannot see your unmarried status lasting for much longer." Christopher took this moment to check the saddle and mount his horse. "I will add that I will happily accept any matrimonial requests for my sister, have them forwarded to Grayson House."

Victoria turned away from her brother.

With a final wave of goodbye, Christopher and Albee touched the brims of their hats, urged their horses forward, and left.

Mrs. Peckover oversaw the initial group of guests the next morning. Miss Lucy Carter was the first to enter Kennington House. Emmeline was immediately notified of Miss Carter's presence and sent the reply, "I will be down in a few minutes."

Some ten minutes later, Miss Hester Enfield arrived. She joined Miss Carter in the front parlor. The two chatted away while Emmeline, still in her bedchamber, continued her morning toilette and a second message was relayed, "I will be down in a few minutes."

Another twenty minutes passed and Miss Teresa Danvers joined the other two. Emmeline was notified of her third visitor and sent a subsequent message to her visitors, "I will be there soon."

Miss Danvers was happy to greet Miss Carter and Miss Enfield, but it was pointed out by Miss Danvers' chaperone that her charge 'cannot occupy a room that contained such a profusion of flowers' as they would cause her to sneeze, quite violently.

Thus the three ladies were relocated to the music room. With the approval of Lady Kennington, Mrs. Peckover had a tea tray sent in with an assortment of biscuits to occupy them while they waited. The three young ladies chatted, discussing the latest fashion, exchanging the names of newly arrived gentlemen they had met, strengthening their budding friendships.

At some point, Lady Amelia Luce appeared at the doorway, gladly joining the young ladies.

"We've been waiting—" Miss Carter thought better of specifying the exact amount of time and merely said, "for a bit."

"It is the precise reason that I delayed my arrival," Lady Amelia enlightened them. "If I am the last visitor, I daresay I shan't need wait too much longer to see Em."

"But you've missed out on the most delicious ginger biscuits," Miss Enfield pointed at the near-empty plate.

"That is a sacrifice I'm willing to endure." Lady Amelia pinched the handle of her teacup, lifted her saucer, then scrutinized what remained on the plate.

The four young ladies did not seem to notice the passage of time as they waited for Lady Emmeline. Amelia, Lucy, Hester, and Teresa, huddled together and chatted, enjoying themselves immensely. They decided that Lady Emmeline was the most charming and most beautiful of them all, no matter her tendency to make her guests wait. The rest of them were merely hanger-oners. Their jubilant voices echoed about the empty music room and down the corridor.

"Whatever are you doing in here?" Emmeline arrived at the open doors looking quite cross yet lovely. "I feel as if I've spent the last hour looking for all of you."

EM SPENT A DELIGHTFUL HALF-HOUR WITH HER VISITORS. AFTER their short visit, one by one, they left, to continue their round of morning calls. All except for Miss Danvers...Teresa.

"Lady Emmeline," Miss Danvers murmured with a shyness Em had not seen earlier. There was something about her demeanor, not joy-filled as it had been when everyone was together but now...she sounded very serious. "I had hoped to have a word with you...alone."

"Very well, Miss Danvers." Em stepped from the foyer into the parlor so they might be private. "Would you care to sit?"

Miss Danvers stopped at the door and sniffed then sneezed. Of course, Em knew her friend was very sensitive to floral scents, she immediately regretted her lapse in memory.

"The flowers! I do beg your pardon," Em apologized.

Miss Danvers sneezed again.

"Goodness, are you quite all right?" Em proffered her delicately embroidered handkerchief and held it out.

"No, thank you. I have one—" A much more *durable* equivalent appeared, catching the subsequent, not so delicate, sneeze. Miss Danvers stepped away from the door, moving back into the foyer.

"Let us remove to the small sitting room, we shall be more comfortable there." Em led the way. Returning to the large music room, on the other side of the house, would prove to be inconvenient. "Let us sit here."

Miss Danvers sat, but she appeared far from comfortable. She still blotted her nose but Em was not sure if the application of her handkerchief was due to the sneeze or if it was something else.

"What is it?" Em suspected the latter.

Teresa Danvers stared helplessly from behind her handkerchief as if she were hiding. "Lady Emmeline, I daresay I *beg* you, please."

Em had no idea to what she referred or what could have brought this on.

"Do not take Lord Hoswell from me." Teresa broke into tears and did not bother to wipe them from her face.

"*Take* him?"

"He told me he loved me. He told me he wished to marry me."

"What's this you say?" Was this the same Lord Hoswell who was to take Em for a drive in the Park this very afternoon?

"He had intended to speak to my father...to...to...." She made quite a watering pot of herself.

"Miss Danvers, please." Em could see her guest was very upset, she hoped, not inconsolable.

"You can have any gentleman in Town, anyone you want—all you need do is smile at them. *Joshua* is the only one I truly care for."

"Is there an *understanding* between you and Lord Hoswell?" Em hadn't heard anything that led her to believe it. She then began to wonder if she *had* stolen him.

"I *thought*...." Miss Danvers nodded between blotting her nose and sniffing. "I thought we had. Then you came along and...and.... Well, look at me." She lowered her hand from her face, resting them in her lap. "I cannot compare to you. You are *beautiful*...a diamond of the first water."

Miss Danvers, with her middling-brown hair and her middling-brown eyes...much like that of a common country mouse. Her physical attributes could not compare to Em's shiny, golden-streaked auburn tresses, thick, long curly lashes, and sparkling brown eyes. She knew it to be true and had always been the celebrated beauty. There was no comparing them.

"I thought if you...if you could only...turn him away he might come back to me."

Em could not like this line of thinking. "Even if that were true...if Lord Hoswell has done such a thing...he is a rude, unthinking bore. I most certainly will turn him away—and I suggest you do the same."

"But I love him." Miss Danvers sounded desperate.

"You need someone who considers your feelings, your needs above their own. He is not worthy of you, Miss Danvers, and I have decided that I shall not have him. His lordship will be handed the mitten upon our next meeting and receive the cut direct from me should our paths cross in the future," Em declared. "And I advise you to do the same."

Admittedly, Miss Danvers, at present, did not look her best. Her red-rimmed, puffy eyes, swollen, drippy nose, and quivering, turned down mouth were not her normal appearance.

However, exterior beauty was not everything—this applied to males as well as females. Beauty tended to attract men but sometimes it was for the wrong reason.

This was so very vexing. Em stood and stomped her foot. Lord Hoswell must have admired something about Miss Danvers to pay her such marked attention.

"I am sure you have fine qualities and have many accomplishments to recommend you." Em laid her hand upon Miss Danvers' arm to lend her some comfort. "You must push his lordship entirely from your mind. There will be another young man who is more suitable and far more agreeable."

Em glanced away thinking of his lordship's previous words and actions to her. He had never indicated he had interests in any other quarter. She stamped her foot again and uttered a soft, exasperated, "Rude!"

ten

THAT NEXT AFTERNOON AT Grayson House, Pauline stood with Jane in the foyer to welcome Lady Frances Abbott and her mother, Lady Langford.

"Please come in, ladies." Jane welcomed her guests.

"I thank you for your invitation, Miss Stiles," Lady Langford uttered. "I'm afraid we were delayed a bit and I worried we might be late."

"You need not concern yourself on that account. I have it on very good authority that you will not be the last ones to arrive." Jane glanced at Pauline.

"It is most kind of you to include us since our association has not been long," Lady Langford replied in a most gracious manner. "As you may understand that we have found invitations are rather thin nowadays."

"Think nothing of it. I am too happy that ours was accepted." Jane nodded to Lady Frances, acknowledging her as well as her mother. "My only wish is for you to be comfortable in our company."

"Miss Stiles, you are a most considerate hostess." Lady Frances smiled at both young ladies.

"Let's not keep our guests standing in the foyer, Miss Jane," Mrs. Heffelfinger whispered, guiding her niece with a gentle reminder. "You can make introductions in the parlor."

Jane's face flushed at the momentary *faux pas* and led them from the foyer. "Oh, yes, you're quite right." She turned to the guests. "I beg your pardon...shall we continue to the parlor and be seated?"

It was entirely understandable. Pauline very well might have made the same mistake herself and blushed along with her friend.

Arriving in the parlor, Jane sent for a tea tray then made introductions. The guests settled into their seats. Not too much time passed before something or someone caught Lady Langford's attention in the corridor.

"If you will excuse me," Lady Langford stood and announced, "I believe my presence is requested elsewhere."

To Pauline, it sounded like an excuse, a well-planned escape in collusion with the other older ladies to leave the young people's company.

The remaining three young ladies sat quietly for some minutes more until Pauline, after daintily clearing her throat, spoke. "As Jane...Miss Stiles and I are the best of friends.... We have recently experienced some *disruption* in our families."

"I am sorry to hear that." Lady Frances' polite remark sounded so selfless to Pauline and she thought the earl's daughter brave.

"I wish to offer my condolences on the loss of your engagement. My brother Martin has had the exact same fate. He and Jane's sister Victoria have decided they don't suit."

"Certainly there is more to it than that," Lady Frances

replied. "A broken engagement may have been the result but there was no telling what had happened between the two. Their differences may have precipitated the duel itself."

Lady Frances might have been correct. "I want you to know that all of our families have been affected, rest assured, you do not suffer alone," Pauline concluded.

"Please do not allow my circumstances to add to your distress," Lady Frances replied, sounding absolutely unaffected. "I must admit that I am not entirely sorry."

Both Pauline and Jane gasped just as a maid arrived with the tea tray. They remained quiet and did not make a sound until the maid withdrew from the room, once again leaving the three alone.

"What is that you say, *Cousin?*" Jane caught herself and amended, "If I may call you cousin?" She took a few minutes to calm herself, enough to fill the teacups for each of them.

"I think that might be permissible...although we are not well-acquainted, we are related," Lady Frances admitted. Apparently, she did not mind Jane's familiar reference.

"How can you be *not* sorry? Do you not care for...for...." Jane continued her questioning and came to a halt when words failed.

"Sir Russell Crawford." Lady Frances spoke without anxiety as she told them of her past. "It was a match my parents, and his, wanted, not I."

"Really?" Jane and Pauline chorused, seemingly equally astonished.

"Sir Russell has been all that is kind, and I believe he genuinely cared for me, but I cannot say that I truly *wished* to marry him." Lady Frances paused and her gaze drifted away. Did she regret confiding in the two young ladies whom she did not know well? "He was not my choice. However, I found him most agreeable."

"The Season has barely begun! I'm certain there are many more suitors for you." Pauline could not believe this earl's daughter did not want for attention from any gentlemen.

"But it has been three years since I was first engaged...since my first Season," Lady Frances stared down into her teacup.

"You were engaged *before* Sir Russell?" Jane, who glanced at Pauline, shared the surprise at the news.

"Yes," Lady Frances admitted rather hesitantly. Perhaps she did regret speaking of such things.

"You are among friends and family here. You may feel free to say what you wish." Pauline set her cup and saucer aside. There was no telling what Lady Frances might say next and Pauline, for one, did not wish to spill her tea.

"I do not think I had the opportunity...." Lady Frances blinked back the moisture gathering in her eyes. "Forgive me. I am very bad to behave so."

"What do you mean?" Pauline was very curious but in no position to pose any questions Jane might as a relation could do.

"If you feel as I had when I was sixteen or seventeen and looking forward to my first Season. I don't think either one of you have reached that age as of yet."

"No," Jane answered, and Pauline shook her head confirming she had not reached that majority either.

"One dreams of their first Season. It is exciting. The new gowns, the parties, the people, is it not? And one meets someone, a man, and thinks she cares for him, for how can one know one is truly in love when one has so little experience with such things?"

"But you did meet someone," Pauline ventured.

"Yes, I did."

"And you agreed to marry him," Jane continued, hoping as Pauline did, that a truthful answer would be forthcoming.

"Yes."

"But what happened?" Pauline could not help herself, she wanted to know.

"I had high hopes for Lord Adolphus. He was amiable and kind."

"And handsome?" Jane encouraged her cousin.

"Oh, yes. He was very handsome." Lady Frances' wistful smile told of her hopes of a bright future for the two of them. "When we agreed to marry he requested we wait until after the Season's end."

"That does not sound unreasonable." Pauline added, "Martin and Victoria delayed their nuptials, planning to wed this year instead of rushing into marriage after last Season."

"True, I did not think it unreasonable either, but after the subsequent Season ended, he requested we further delay our ceremony until sometime the following year. We were well into the year when he asked to postpone our wedding a second time. I refused, waiting two years was very far beyond the pale."

"That was...very bad of him." Pauline could not have agreed more.

"I did not understand his reasons. If he did not wish to marry me, he should have never asked."

"It was completely inconsiderate." Jane, of course, saw the sense in her cousin's actions.

"Now I've returned two years later and two years older." Lady Frances shook her head. "I'm afraid I may find myself at somewhat of a disadvantage."

"Only two years?" Jane could not believe it. "That is *nothing*."

"If one were to wait when one is fourteen until one is sixteen, it is nothing. But I was seventeen and now I am now nineteen, nearing twenty, almost on the shelf."

The admission left the young ladies in shock. Pauline was very glad she had not been holding her teacup.

Lady Frances continued her tale. "During my first Season, there was another young man who had shown interest in me."

"Was it Sir Russell, then?" Jane guessed.

"He wrote to me when he learned I had not wed—was no longer engaged to be married, and he begged me to write to him."

"Sir Russell...." Pauline echoed.

"Perhaps it was his interest that gave me the strength to refuse Lord Adolphus. It was after months of correspondence, encouragement from my siblings, and both our parents. When I was free from my previous commitment, Sir Russell proposed, and I accepted...conditionally."

Pauline and Jane sighed. Her tale promised a romantic ending and the young ladies hung onto every word.

"It was agreed we would meet once the Season began and if we still felt as we had all those months ago, we would announce our engagement."

Both young ladies knew what had happened to that pending announcement—it had vanished.

"A few days ago my parents received a letter from Lord and Lady Emerson informing them that the engagement was canceled."

Pauline brought her hand to her mouth, suppressing her gasp.

"I cannot imagine...you must have been devastated." Jane pressed her hands together.

"As I said Sir Russell was more my parents' choice than mine. I understand they would wish me to make a match this

Season. If I had not, well...I would feel sorry for my younger sisters. What opportunities would they have if I do not make a successful marriage?"

"But you are an earl's daughter, surely that must make some difference." Neither Jane nor Pauline would have the benefit of her elevated social position.

"I am an earl's *eldest* daughter. It's best if one has youth and looks. If one waits too long, the opportunity may be lost."

With that said the sound of the front door opening and voices drew the ladies' attention.

"Please excuse me." Jane rose to greet their final guests. "Lady Emmeline and her mother have arrived."

"Lady Langford. Lady Frances." As the young hostess, Cousin Jane made the introductions. "May I present Lady Kennington and her daughter, Lady Emmeline?"

A round of 'How do you do?' swept through the room as the two mothers and daughters greeted one another. What she could not comprehend was just how lovely Lady Emmeline was. Truly lovely in grace and stature. Was this the appearance of every girl coming out for their first Season? Lady Emmeline made Frances feel quite the antidote in comparison.

Growing up she must have had every advantage and because of her position, she would have been schooled in similar manners and accomplishments as Frances. What musical instrument did Lady Emmeline play? Could she sing well? Did she paint? What of her skill with a needle? Was she well-read? Did she read poetry?

Frances thought this young lady would have every best opportunity the Season had to offer. How could the gentlemen not fall over themselves to catch her eye? And how every young lady would wish to be in her good graces and have the pleasure of calling her *friend*.

Mrs. Chandler emerged from the corridor, greeting, "Lady Kennington—finally!"

"I do apologize if we are a bit late." Lady Emmeline's voice sounded like lilting music and she was without a doubt the loveliest creature Frances had ever beheld.

"Are you late?" Frances nearly forgot they had been waiting for the last guests to arrive.

"Maybe just a bit. Lord Hoswell simply would not allow me to depart. He was quite insistent that I remain at his side, which was wholly impossible." A slight flush of pink washed across Lady Emmeline's cheeks in the most attractive manner. "His behavior was most improper."

Someone coughed.

"Shall we find our table and begin?" Cousin Jane suggested. "The elder ladies have removed to the dining room to play their game, far enough distance, I dare say."

"I am glad we need not be concerned that we will be overheard." Lady Emmeline appeared to be a bit overly worried at the prospect, for some reason unknown to Frances.

"Only this time we intend to play cards, do we not, Jane?" Miss Chandler wondered.

"Oh yes, for this is a *proper* card party," Cousin Jane informed all of them. She led the way into the parlor.

"But there will be time to share a bit of gossip, won't there?" Lady Emmeline whispered in what Frances imagined was her most enticing manner as to heighten their curiosity. "I have heard some interesting tidbits from a party I attended the other night."

"*Gossip*?" Frances' hopes for having Lady Emmeline as a

friend dissolved. "I really do not care for gossip." It was mostly because she did not care to be discussed.

"I'm sure there will be enough time for both," Cousin Jane said in an amicable manner and motioned that they be seated.

"This is, after all, a ladies' party."

"Let us play a few hands, shall we?" Cousin Jane slid the deck to Frances. "Newest guests have the honor of first deal."

Frances shuffled the cards, glanced up at the ladies seated at the table, and asked, "What shall we play?"

THANKFULLY THERE WAS MORE CARD PLAY THAN TALK AMONGST the young ladies. Jane had enjoyed taking part in the previous gossip they shared but had hoped for less on that front, and thought her first party was so far a success. Lady Emmeline whispered bits of Town news while the cards were shuffled and dealt. This impressed Jane and Pauline but Cousin Frances did not seem to care for it at all.

A knock on the front door brought a halt to their game. No one else had been expected.

Male voices filled the air, sending the young ladies into not-so-silent hysterics. Liddell was doing his utmost to persuade them the inhabitants were not At Home. The butler could not be held accountable, Jane's guests could not remain silent.

Their giggles gave themselves away. Remaining quiet was impossible and there was no use pretending they were not there, she laid her cards face down on the table and motioned to the other three to follow her. Jane noticed her Cousin Frances opted to remain at the table.

"Miss Stiles!" Viscount Epping called out to her, rather inelegantly, she thought. The young men helped themselves into the front parlor, without being invited, where they met up with the young ladies.

"Nicky! What are you doing here?" Lady Emmeline sounded outraged with her brother's presence.

"*Ma* friends and I were calling on Miss Stiles," he remarked rather snobbishly, turning a shoulder in her direction.

"All *three* of you?" Lady Emmeline must have thought along the same lines as Jane, believing them to be somewhat overzealous.

"That's right," he replied. All three young men nodded in agreement thinking nothing odd about their situation, or their behavior.

"You may perhaps wish to consult an etiquette book regarding Morning Calls." Lady Emmeline's nose lifted a bit as she spoke.

"No idea you were here too, Em."

"Pardon me, my lady," Sir John remarked. "We don't abide by those rules really."

"Obviously not," Lady Emmeline retorted. "That is what happens when Eton boys are set loose at the end of term."

"Beg pardon," Mr. Newbury put in with a smile. "We attend Oxford now."

"Yes, that's right. We came to pay Miss Stiles a Morning Call and we were hoping, if we were fortunate enough, to make your brother's acquaintance." Lord Epping did the talking, the other two glanced about in hopes of catching sight of Kit.

Mrs. Heffelfinger appeared at the parlor doors. "Sir Christopher is not currently At Home," she informed them in stern tones.

"Oh, that's too bad," Mr. Newbury appeared a bit disappointed at the news. The other two appeared equally as dismayed.

It was quite lowering to think one's brother held more interest for a young gentleman caller than the young lady who was the stated reason for their call.

"I personally wanted to tell him that Lord Keene dueled Sir Jeremy Hunt this very morning over a splendid waistcoat made by Sir Christopher's tailor if he hadn't heard," Mr. Newbury offered with great excitement. Apparently, *gossip* was not limited to females.

"Christopher's tailor?" Jane did not recall that her brother owned a garment worthy of a duel. She thought that he had unusually good taste.

"Seems Lord Keene took offense to it," Sir John added.

"Over a *waistcoat*?" Pauline remarked as if this were the most ridiculous bit of news.

"I had heard about that." Lady Emmeline glanced skyward as if it were of little consequence and less interest.

"Lord Keene was the noble one who would not allow it to interfere between their friendship and he was the first to delope," Mr. Newbury informed them.

"But there was an injury" —Sir John gave this latest tidbit more of a dramatic delivery— "Not a mortal blow by any means."

Jane hated to think anyone would have been hurt by such ridiculousness.

"Yes," Lord Epping returned to the discussion. "William Hackett."

"He wasn't dueling." Sir John nudged his friend.

"When Sir Jeremy fired his pistol, the ball hit an overhead branch that fell onto a coach that spooked the horses that ran down Hackett."

"Thank goodness there was a surgeon in attendance." Mr. Newbury addressed the group. "He saw to Hackett's injury right away."

"I'll have that Lorenzo-fellow make me one of those waist-coats." Lord Epping stood tall and smoothed his hands down his torso as if preparing to be measured.

"We're all going down there," Mr. Newbury said, indicating Sir John with a jab of his thumb. They'd not be left out.

"For a waistcoat that might get you shot?" Pauline sounded appalled by the notion.

"One can only hope," Lady Emmeline remarked before returning to the parlor.

There was another knock on the front door. Those in the foyer fell silent while Liddell answered. He returned with an envelope. "Miss Stiles?"

The room's occupants stilled and stared at their hostess.

Jane recognized Kit's handwriting. She took the letter, cracked open the seal, and unfolded the single-page letter.

"It's from Sir Christopher," Pauline whispered to the others. The silence lengthened as they waited for the news it contained.

Dearest Jane,

Just a brief note to tell you we have arrived in Bath. Mama and Vic have been delivered into the safe care of Lady Belton. I take the afternoon to rest and will begin my return tomorrow morning.

I travel by horseback. The journey home should be short and I expect to arrive by Friday. If all goes well, I shall have a surprise for you upon my return.

Yrs, Kit

Jane sighed, lowering the missive and turned her head to gaze upon her guests. "He expects to return on Friday."

Friday felt as if it were ages away.

Eleven

"Miss Stiles was so good as to inform me that her brother would arrive today. I told her to expect us first thing in the morning." Lady Langford announced her plans to her daughter and made straight for the corridor. "See that you are ready to accompany me."

"But Mama...it is ten in the morning. You cannot possibly land on someone's doorstep at this hour."

"Sir Christopher is to arrive today and I intend to be there when he does." Lady Langford had already started preparing herself for the journey.

Frances doubted he would arrive first thing in the morning... and what did her mother think she was going to do while she waited? Lady Langford, who was not usually considered a strong, forthright woman, now that she was in this state was not to be stopped. Frances best be prepared to leave for Grayson House. She could make her apology to Jane and Mrs. Heffelfinger when she arrived, and to Sir Christopher, after she had made his acquaintance.

Frances made haste and somehow arrived at the ground

floor as her mother stepped onto the staircase. Continuing into the parlor, to give herself a moment to pull on her gloves, Frances noticed a very impressive arrangement of flowers sitting on the large round foyer table.

"Mama, did you order flowers?" It seemed unusual her parent would do such a thing without expecting visitors or the approach of a party. If Frances had an admirer perhaps...but that was not a topic on which she cared to linger.

"No, dear." Lady Langford answered. "Look for a card."

Frances set her gloves and reticule on the table and walked around the bouquet looking for a card which she found off to one side. It was addressed to her.

What might have been a joyful moment filled her with such dread. She took in a breath, opened the note and read:

My Dearest Lady Frances,

The day you bid me farewell was the worst day of my life. Is it possible you can forgive my bad behavior and allow me to make amends? I have come to Town in hopes that you will reconsider.

Adolphus

Frances did not crumple the note or consign him to the devil. There was no ill-will felt toward Adolphus. Not anymore, too much time had passed. She wanted to get on with her life. She had more important issues with which to deal, as in being set on the shelf.

"Who sent them?" Lady Langford stopped next to her daughter. She sniffed with disgust when she read the signature. "Interesting."

"I have no idea why he would waste his time. He has no chance of regaining my affection." Frances told her parent. After everything he had put her through…after the wasted years…. "I would never take him back."

"I have the feeling he believes it would be such a simple thing." Apparently, Lady Langford wasn't impressed either.

"Simple? *Impossible*, I'd say," Frances admitted.

There was a time she might have reacted differently because she dare not chance losing him. He had been an excellent match…two years ago. But with his reluctance to wed, Frances had had enough. Even her mother's pleas with her to wait 'just a bit longer' fell on deaf ears. It appeared now that Lady Langford was of the same mind as her daughter.

Frances was finished with him and she would not, under any circumstances, bother with him now. She wasn't sure if she would even acknowledge him if she saw him.

"Shall we go?" Her ladyship murmured to her daughter and waved for the butler to open the door. Their coach stood before their house waiting to take on its passengers.

It startled Jane somewhat when Lady Langford stepped through the front door of Grayson House, past the butler without invitation, and without regrets or excuses. Lady Frances quietly followed her mother inside and Liddell closed the door behind them.

"We have been expecting you and have planned to keep you comfortable until such time that Sir Christopher arrives." Mrs. Heffelfinger did not appear put out at the inconvenience and did not display the slightest bit of irritation.

"Please inform him, upon his arrival, that I wait in the library," her ladyship announced.

Mrs. Heffelfinger appeared and motioned to a footman to do as the countess bid.

"Lead the way, my good man." Her ladyship acknowledged Mrs. Heffelfinger with a nod and followed the servant down the corridor, presumably, to the library, leaving her daughter standing in the foyer for Jane to deal with.

"I am so very sorry we've come unannounced, Cousin Jane." Lady Frances appeared mortified at her mother's actions. "You are both so very kind to accommodate us, especially on such short notice."

"I daresay this was not your idea, *Cousin*." Jane would not blame her and would do her best to make Lady Frances feel welcome.

She cast her gaze to the floor, which was answer enough.

"Allow me to take your hat and coat." Jane accepted them with kindness and placed them on the large foyer table.

"You might as well make yourselves comfortable. I'll have a tray sent to the parlor for you ladies, no telling how long you'll be waiting. I need to attend to Lady Langford at once." Mrs. Heffelfinger sounded concerned and left.

Jane and Cousin Frances exchanged strained smiles before heading to the parlor to wait until Kit's arrival...however long that would take.

CHRISTOPHER, WITH ALBEE RIDING BY HIS SIDE, PASSED THE FINAL toll-gate. It would feel good to finally be home without the worry of Victoria's antics. He was eager to return to see Jane, sit at his dining table for a meal, and find a decent night's sleep. He looked forward to Albee's companionship in the coming weeks and introducing him to the many pleasantries that Town offered. There was the promise to Jane of parties—although she was not yet Out, promises had been made, and needed to be kept. There were few close friends and acquaintances to provide enough socialization for her and as it turned out the very same might prove helpful to ease Albee's reentry into Society.

Of course, Jane's friendship with Pauline Chandler would continue regardless of the broken engagement between Victoria and Martin. In the same vein, Christopher still considered Martin one of his best friends and expected that friendship to last.

Perhaps after he and Albee cleaned up, had a rest, and had a bite to eat, they'd pay Martin a visit, and Christopher's two very good friends could become acquainted. If introductions went well, he and his two friends might become a merry three.

Leaving their horses with the stablehands, Christopher and Albee entered Grayson House through the side door. Liddell was there to greet them.

"Welcome home, sir." The butler collected Christopher's hat.

"Thank you, Liddell." The pace in which they rode home, although not quite breakneck, had been fairly brisk as Christopher wanted the travel to be over and done.

"See Mr. Winslow installed in the Green Suite, will you, Liddell?"

"As you wish, sir. I shall see to it at once."

Albee handed over his hat and gloves to the butler with a nod. There was a silent moment before a familiar squeal pierced the air.

"Kit!" Jane came dashing from the parlor and wrapped her arms around him. "You've finally returned!" Her eyes were squeezed closed as she held tight onto her brother.

"This is quite the welcome home." Christopher returned her hug. There was no doubt she would need to change her dress after his hearty welcome. "Don't leave me again, Kit. Ever."

"You know I cannot very well promise that." He managed to extract himself and stepped back from her. "Look what I've done." A distinct transfer of dust had discolored her light-colored calico. "Your dress is filthy."

"What care I of my dress? You are home!" She stepped toward him again and he held her at bay.

"You must allow me time to change and get settled." Christopher spotted Albee not far behind him and went apparently unobserved by Jane. "And after you've done so, please arrange some tea and a good deal of food." He walked her to the staircase and smiled before sending her on her way. "Your surprise will need to be fed."

Jane's eyes went wide with uncertainty.

The butler cleared his throat, gaining Christopher's attention once more. "Sir Christopher, there is an urgent matter that needs your immediate attention."

"Can't it wait?" Christopher had literally stepped off his horse, only moments before, entered the house and hadn't yet finished removing his outer raiment much less his sister's grasp.

"I'm afraid not, sir. Lady Langford has called previously while you were away and is now in the library...since before noon. Her daughter currently waits in the front parlor."

"Now?" Gad, he had been away for only a few days and he couldn't imagine what could have happened to warrant his immediate attention. "I'd best see Lady Langford straightaway then."

"But Kit—" Jane had meant to delay him at any cost.

"Mind your frock, if you please. Go on." Christopher raised his eyebrows, expecting her compliance. "Jane...please."

"Very well." He knew she was unhappy to leave his side but

she did so. Jane sulked up the stairs and took each step in a painfully slow manner.

While watching his sister move out of sight, Christopher peeled off his outerwear and held it in Liddell's direction, hoping it was close enough for the butler to retrieve. He headed down the corridor to the library, quickening his pace in a matter of seconds. The butler caught the coat before it hit the ground, sending a shimmer of dust into the air.

Passing the open doors of the parlor, Christopher paused, catching sight of someone—a young lady—seated on the sofa.

"I beg your pardon, Miss." He performed a quick bow and called out, "Albee! Would you see to—" Kit pointed toward the opened door, to where Albert should venture forth. "I'll leave you two to discover your connection while I see to—" Kit indicated the direction he would be off to and again he dashed off down the corridor.

Not that Albert thought his friend's behavior was odd...but he wondered if this was normal for Kit. The running from London to Bath, and back again—running down the corridor from one side of the house to the other.

Albee strolled down the corridor where Kit had previously traveled that brought him presumably to the front parlor. Inside, stood a young lady. She was dressed in a lovely green morning gown. Her brown hair, curled artfully around her oval face. She had a delicate yet stately bearing.

"I am sorry to disturb you." Albert stopped at the open door and bowed to her. "I have been left with abrupt instructions and a puzzle."

She rose to her feet when he entered.

"I beg you forgive my appearance, ma'am." Albert's outer raiment, left with the butler, was the most of it, but his boots and breeches were covered with dust.

"You are hardly to blame, sir. If I understand correctly you have only arrived after hours of riding a great distance."

"Yes." He chuckled.

"You arrived with Sir Christopher?"

"Yes, just now." He motioned outside, from where he had come.

"And you do not yet have a room to freshen up," the lady so kindly pointed out.

"That is also true. Although one is being prepared as we speak." Albert felt some discomfort that he reeked of horse. Another reason to be grateful for an excuse to address her from the doorway. "And here we stand, neglecting basic etiquette."

There was acceptance in their silence.

The young lady glanced about, perhaps listening for someone to approach. "Miss Stiles has stepped away."

"Uh...I'm afraid I am not as of yet acquainted with Miss Stiles." Albert was beginning to think their circumstance might not have a resolution.

"Shall we call the butler?" This pretty, young lady glanced about, seemingly to find another solution to their dilemma. "I believe we are both known to him."

"I cannot be certain but I do not believe an introduction by a servant is at all considered proper." Albert doubted that would have changed during his absence from Society.

"I suppose you are correct." The young lady stared beyond him, in the direction where he had last seen Kit and the butler.

"However, as unconventional as performing one's introductions may be, Sir Christopher implied there was a familial connection between us." How wrong could introducing oneself to one's relation be?

"You might be correct that we break with convention—we

are at an impasse." She paused then offered him a smile. "Please, sir, I beg that you proceed."

"Very well." Albert, still standing in the corridor, and hopefully downwind, "I am Mr. Albert Winslow of Wells, Somerset." He bowed trying to raise as little dust as possible.

"I am Lady Frances Abbott, daughter of the Earl and Countess of Langford." Lady Frances curtsied.

"Ah, Lady Langford...." He mouthed, having heard that name a few minutes ago. Kit had been summoned by Lady Frances' mother.

"Yes, exactly." Lady Frances inclined her head. "How do you do, Mr. Winslow?"

"How do you do?" Albert smiled. This was Lady Langford's lovely daughter. The knowledge of her name after their unseemly introduction to one another calmed him immensely.

twelve

"Now that we have taken care of our introductions, can we not be comfortable?" Mr. Winslow bowed and gestured toward the sofa where Frances previously sat before his arrival. He was remarkably well-turned-out for someone who had just spent hours in a saddle, Mr. Winslow did not appear as disheveled as he might. His smile, whenever he chose to display it, seemed to eliminate any weariness from his face.

"If I understand correctly, I believe Sir Christopher is currently occupied with your mother. I have no idea how long we could be left standing."

"Very well, Mr. Winslow." Frances retook her seat and Mr. Winslow hesitantly entered the parlor and lowered himself in a chair, keeping his distance. Clearly she felt very uncomfortable, he may have felt the same. He ran his hand over his light-brown, wavy hair, rearranging his locks that had been crushed by his hat.

"I suppose I cannot blame Sir Christopher for his lack of introductions. He was quite in a rush—if that was indeed Sir

Christopher who passed by, I have yet to make his acquaintance. My mother is to blame, I fear, not he."

"I admit, he is not usually so abrupt." Mr. Winslow defended his friend. "Kit must have been in a hurry, indeed. This is most irregular."

Frances had no idea what she should say to the newcomer. She felt uncomfortable in their situation and could not even offer him refreshment since this was not her house. Here she sat with a stranger in a strange house for who knows how long? How awkward this was—for both of them.

"Perhaps we should do as Sir Christopher's suggested and discover our connection?" Mr. Winslow displayed a most confident bearing and did not appear inconvenienced. "Would you care to delineate your lineage first or shall I?"

"Please, feel free to begin," Frances said with a nod.

"Let's see.... I met Sir Christopher in my youth at Eton, we were very good friends at the time. A few years later, upon our return from term break, it seemed his mother, now Lady Yardley, married my uncle Lord Beeson." Mr. Winslow tilted his head toward her and narrowed his eyes in thought. "Who was on my mother's side and that marriage made him my cousin."

"Ah. I see," Frances replied. "Well, Sir Christopher's half-sister Victoria Abbott is my first cousin" —Frances nodded her head as if that could indicate one side of her family tree— "On my father's side. Which makes my father, the Earl of Langford, Miss Abbott's uncle."

"Then it seems," Mr. Winslow continued, "We are cousins by marriage...or should I say...*marriages*."

"So...." Frances ventured to make a guess. "That would make us *cousins* of some sort."

"Uh...yes, I believe it would." He glanced in her direction, giving her an excellent view of his profile with his straight nose and his strong jawline. "Not by blood and not very close cousins at that as there are several marriages in there."

"Exactly how many times has Lady Yardley been married?" Frances had no wish to pry into Sir Christopher's personal matters but she was curious now that they were discussing the topic of his family history.

"I just learned this very thing yesterday." Mr. Winslow pressed his hands together and splayed his fingers when he said, "Lady Yardley's marriage comes to a total of ten, I believe."

"Ten!" The number horrified her. Ten marriages, ten husbands—and here Frances could not secure one.

"To be honest, I believe her appearance is not of a mother but more as an elder sister to her brood. She still appears remarkably youthful," he told her. "It's not the ten marriages that surprise me, it's the dozen children she's had."

"A dozen!" That number was not quite as shocking considering the ten marriages.

"All boys except for two girls."

"Victoria and Jane." Frances knew that much. "Knowing Sir Christopher for as long as you have, I suppose you are fairly well-versed with Lady Yardley's family."

"You might have thought that but a few years back Kit and I lost touch—" his voice held a tinge of sadness.

Something unfortunate must have happened and Frances did not feel she knew this man well enough to ask.

"By some strange happenstance, we had been brought together in Bath, at my aunt's house."

"I understand he escorted his mother and his sister Victoria in what may be described as an exile," Frances commented.

"I suppose you could call it that."

By the tone of each, it was clear they both knew they touched on a delicate topic that neither wished to elaborate.

Remaining vague worked for both of them and it would not have been out of the question to believe he knew relatively the same details as she.

Sir Christopher Glory entered the library where he found Lady Langford sitting comfortably occupied with a book and a cup of tea.

"Pray forgive me for making you wait, Lady Langford." He bowed upon entering and approached her.

She gazed at him over her lorgnette, taking in his person standing before her. "I can see you've only just arrived, so *you* have not made me wait long." Setting the book to one side on the table, her ladyship straightened in her chair to address him.

Lady Langford sat wrapped comfortably in a shawl having removed her hat and gloves upon her arrival many hours before. It appeared she had made preparations to remain for as long as it took to wait for his return.

"I know we must have met previously but I'm afraid I do not recall making your acquaintance." Christopher recognized her as family but could not speak to her with the same familiarity a close blood connection would normally allow.

"I believe you were quite young when we first met. I doubt you would remember. I am surprised that I am known to you at all."

"Yes, you are, ma'am. I make it my business to know all the members of my family. Some find it a monumental task that I've undertaken." He hoped he was paying her due respect. She outranked him in class and age. "As I understand it your initial call to Grayson House was days ago while I was away."

"I thought you might have left Town for good."

"Not at all. My brief absence was only to settle Lady Yardley and my sister Victoria in Bath after the" —He glanced downward, feeling a bit timid regarding the reasons why the trip was necessary. It most probably was no longer a secret, and to speak its name, no longer shocking— "Unpleasantness of the duel."

"Is that what you call it, *unpleasantness?* Did you not think what your actions would do to others?" She lowered her eyewear, folded them, and laid them on her book.

"My only consideration was what Society dictated. It was expected that I should uphold the honor of my sister. I cannot say what I did was *right*, all I can say is...I performed my duty."

"*Your* duty, for the honor of your sister? You have ruined my Frances' engagement and most probably her chances for making another suitable match. Do you not realize she came out three years ago? She has had two failed engagements and she is practically on the shelf."

He didn't need to hear this. Christopher moved to a tall side table and filled a glass from a decanter. He needed a little liquid to wash the dust from his throat and bring focus to his mind.

"How does that compare to my sister who is most probably *ruined* and also faces a failed engagement, be it only one, and has no prospects for a match?" While holding his glass in one hand, with his other he carefully replaced the stopper in the decanter.

"*Dear God!*" Lady Langford cried out, stretching her arm in an attempt to maintain balance while seated at his shocking words.

Christopher glanced in her direction, considering if he need come to her aid. He recognized a fit of the vapors when he saw it and decided to remain where he stood. As her ladyship was seated, she would not have fallen far had she swooned. Instead, he took the two small steps near her and silently offered his untouched glass, moving it toward her empty, outstretched hand. It appeared she needed it more than he.

"No, thank you. I—" She started to refuse but changed her mind, taking hold of the cut-crystal tumbler. "Thank you."

Returning to the side table, he poured himself another. He downed its contents in two quick swallows while she lingered over the rim of her glass. "What would you have me do, my lady?"

Lady Langford was obviously displeased with him. And how would he make amends? Was it even possible?

"*Do*? Haven't you done enough?" With both hands, she brought the edge of the glass to her lips and sipped. Her sound of displeasure at tasting the spirits he thought satisfactory told him it was not her usual habit to imbibe.

"You must have some purpose for coming here. Was it to scold me? Surely those in Society will do far worse." He paused and allowed the silence to seep between them while he refilled his glass.

"I do not know if there is anything you can do, Sir Christopher." She sniffed becoming emotional—it could not have been caused by the alcohol. "It is not only Frances but there are her two younger sisters." She sniffed again. "What is to become of them? How will they ever make a successful match with their sister's shame?" Lady Langford must have felt a bout of tears coming on for she tugged at a handkerchief from the wrist of her sleeve.

"I also have a younger sister I must consider." He did not wish to think about Jane's fate now. "I am sure there will be whispers she may not hear and a shadow that she may not be able to escape."

Lady Langford sniffed again, perhaps this time it was for Jane as well as her own daughter.

Christopher pushed a footstool closer to my lady's chair and sat before her. His intent was to comfort her and he spoke in a soft voice.

"The duel was required. I had no wish to harm anyone. Lord Linwood, Lady Frances, or me...however, the outcome now sees Lady Yardley, Victoria, and Lord Linwood all in exile. Currently, my family, which includes you and Lady Frances, stand on the brink of scandal." He touched her trembling arm while she pressed her handkerchief to her cheek. "I apologize for the harm I have caused. You must understand I did what I thought best."

The one thing Christopher did not know was how all this affected him. Would *he* be shunned when he faced Society? Would they turn their backs on *him* because he dared to uphold the honor of his sister, only to delope? There would be only one way to find out.

"I believe there may be something I can do." And only one way to discover if there was something to be done about helping Lady Frances.

Lady Langford stared at him with hope-filled eyes.

"I have only returned this afternoon but if you will allow me to attend a party this evening and ascertain if I have garnered any public animosity. If I am shunned outright then—" Christopher noted the fear in her eyes at the very prospect. "We shall see, shall we?" He tried to sound positive but did not hold much hope there would be a favorable outcome.

"Very well." Lady Langford wiped under both her eyes and inhaled deeply, regaining her composure.

"Will you wait to hear from me? All I ask is that you remain calm and do nothing."

She nodded. "And you will call tomorrow morning?"

"Yes, I promise."

With a final sniff, Lady Langford, now fully poised, stood,

ready to leave. She returned her handkerchief to the wrist of her sleeve, set the glass on the table, and took up her book and lorgnette, before moving to the library door.

With her back still to him, she spoke. "Thank you, Sir Christopher. You are indeed your mother's son." And with those kind words, she left.

"ARE YOU CERTAIN WE SHOULD ATTEND TONIGHT?" THEY HAD ONLY arrived in Town and Albert wasn't certain he was ready to step out into Society so soon. He gazed around the spacious entry hall of the grand Mayfair residence. "Whose house is this again?"

Kit leaned to his right to whisper, "We are at the home of the Duke and Duchess of Calvert."

"Right." This was hardly the *easing* into Society Albert had imagined. This felt as if he had been tossed headlong into the fire. He only agreed to attend to keep Kit company.

"I made a promise," Kit reminded him.

"I promised nothing," Albert maintained.

"But you would not allow me to suffer on my own, would you?"

"I would not but more fool me." No, Albert would not allow Kit to descend into Hades alone. Calvert House might very well be a viper's den. He nor Kit had knowledge of what lay ahead but they would find out together, and very soon.

"It's been a long time since I've worn dress breeches." The jacket was none too comfortable either, a bit snug fitting for him.

"It's been a long time since you've stepped off your estate," Kit commented. "There was no need while you were rusticating."

"No, there wasn't. I was very comfortable there." Albert just hoped there would be no dancing involved tonight. He was woefully out of practice.

"Sometimes it is good to step into the unknown." Kit could not have sounded more unsure of that.

"I do not believe I could drift further from my element than here." The surrounding shine and elegance were unfamiliar from his normal rustic country abode.

"Shall we see what awaits us?" Kit led the way and Albert positioned himself just behind his friend's right shoulder where he would remain close yet it would give him a good vantage point.

Kit walked forward, making his way to the ballroom.

"My dear Sir Christopher!" one man greeted as jolly as Albert had ever heard. "How good it is to see you. I somehow thought that you had fled after that noble deed on the field. You shouldn't have spared that rascal Linwood, you know."

Kit, who did not react surprised, stopped to respond to the man. "You don't think so, Roland?"

"Should have put the ball clean through him." Roland expounded, feeling rather strongly about it.

"I hardly think it warranted. Lord Linwood was only expressing his opinion," Kit replied. "And I do not think my sister's reputation is worth another man's life."

"True, true," he mused.

"Sir Christopher!" A second man called to him. "You have been too kind to Linwood. The rogue deserved to die!"

"Come, Morris, that's a bit harsh, ain't it?" Kit's bantering came quick and easy. Clearly, this was not the disdain he had expected, that must have been good news.

"Not sayin' what he said ain't true, mind. Yours was a heroic deed. Upholding the virtue of your sister might have cost you your life."

"I hardly think I was in danger from Linwood. That man can't hit the north side of Carlton House." Kit nudged Morris. "Tell me, am I welcome here? Or should I pack my bags and go back to Barlow Hall?"

"*Welcome*?" Morris chuckled. "I think you'll find you're more than welcome. They'll be those who'll want to shake your hand for how you handled the entire incident."

"For what? Deloping?" Kit sent Albert an unsettled glance.

"Shouldn't have, is what I'm saying. I'm not the only one who thinks that." Morris made a sweeping gesture, encompassing everyone.

"You are collecting some notice," Albert pointed out.

"What?" Kit must not have realized he was becoming the center of attention. Other guests were gathering around and congratulating him.

"Here is the gentleman himself," a voice called out upon spotting Sir Christopher.

"Join us, Harrison!" Morris called out, waving over another acquaintance.

"Did you hear about the duel the other morning?" Harrison wanted to add another story to the dueling tales.

"Yes, I had heard," Walton replied. "It was over a waistcoat, made by Lorenzo, I believe."

"That's my tailor," Kit confirmed.

"Yes, he had it made because the man *was* your tailor," Harrison affirmed.

"Was it one of those horrid things, such as the one you wore?" Albert asked. "The one that made me feel ill?"

"Heard it made Lord Keene dizzy...nauseous really. They had to settle the whole thing on the field," Walton explained.

"Anyone hurt?" The idea horrified Albert.

"No, they both deloped. It was the silliest thing." Walton shrugged. It appeared he thought the whole exercise was futile. "Nothing noble about that."

"That's not right. And did you know...Hackett was nearly trampled by horses." Morris punctuated the tragedy with the stab of his index finger.

"At the duel?"

"It wasn't a horse race, you know. Nasty business, that." Walton shook his head. "Good on you, Sir Christopher."

"There was another duel this morning...." A man's voice, coming from behind them rose above the others. He must have not heard the news they had discussed. "Do tell me, dear sir." He worked his way through the crowd toward Morris' side.

Kit turned his back and brought Albert to the center of their group. "By-the-bye, gentlemen. I wish to make you known to my friend Mr. Albert Winslow who has recently returned to Town."

With a mixture of varying acknowledgments thrown his way, Albert thought the introduction was not in any way adequate. He caught a handful of the gentlemen's names as Kit called them out.

"Come, Albee, let us continue." Kit clapped him on the shoulder to urge him forward.

Another, "Well done, Sir Christopher!" was called out as they walked from the entryway to the corridor just outside the ballroom.

By the time they made it to the ballroom, everyone knew Sir Christopher Glory had returned to London. Considering the jubilant expressions and encouraging cheers, all were glad to see him.

This was no viper's den, Albert thought, this gathering was more admiration of a champion, ready to raise Kit onto a plinth.

thirteen

"Lady Langford awaits you in her sitting room, Sir Christopher."

The visitor shed his hat and gloves upon entering Langford House, leaving them with the butler before following him down the corridor. Step after step, Christopher felt the house stood quiet around him as if it were in mourning.

The two men came to a stop and the butler turned about and gestured for the visitor to continue into the room.

"Sir Christopher," Lady Langford greeted him. "I am glad to see you at such an early hour, you have not kept me waiting all day to hear your news. Will you please be seated?"

"Thank you, my lady." He made himself comfortable in a chair next to her. This would be a discussion regarding good news, although he did not think it would take long, but one never knew.

"Tell me what it is you have discovered." Her focus upon him was intense.

"I am happy to say I was most welcomed at the Calvert party last night."

The expression of relief and delight lit her face. The tightness in her shoulders relaxed and Kit heard an audible sigh from her ladyship.

"I might even say there exists a bit of hero worship taking place."

"Hero worship?" Lady Langford sounded intrigued.

"I have heard since my absence there have been other duels occurring where the participants have deloped by design. I am led to believe they are in some way mimicking my behavior."

"I'm not certain I understand you."

"It is a ridiculous notion, I must admit." He shook his head, unable to fully comprehend why anyone would care to reenact something that was potentially so very dangerous. "It is as if somehow, I was to be highly admired for allowing Lord Linwood to live."

"Has nothing been said of Miss Abbott? The tarnish to her reputation?"

"Not that I had heard, ma'am. If there is no scandal, do you believe Lady Frances' engagement might still stand?"

"I'm not certain. I would need to consult with Lord and Lady Emerson on the matter. However, I do believe Sir Russell would be most amenable." Lady Langford sounded as if there were some hope for her daughter after all. "He is so very fond of her."

"If I might make a suggestion...."

"And what is that?" Her ladyship appeared open to what he might have to say, which surprised him.

"If I might escort Lady Frances tonight, she may benefit from being seen in public with me." He had not phrased that quite right but it essentially was what he meant. "Where is she now?"

"Out for a walk with her maid. Frances has been cooped up inside for nearly a week, poor thing just wanted a breath of air."

"I briefly saw her yesterday." Christopher remembered

dashing by the front parlor and seeing a young lady inside. "Didn't even have time to speak to her or for a proper introduction."

"There will be time enough for that." Lady Langford nodded, making up her mind on what was to be done. "If you are willing to provide an escort, I will make certain she is ready this evening."

FRANCES AND HER LADY'S MAID SAUNDERS WALKED SIDE BY SIDE through Grosvenor Square taking the air.

"It does feel good to be outdoors, doesn't it, child?"

Child? Frances glanced at her maid and wondered how she could be referred to as a *child* when she was near twenty years of age?

"I have heard her ladyship tell his lordship of your visit to Grayson House." Saunders could not have been much older than Frances herself but behave as if she had added a mere ten years to her age. "You'll see. Sir Christopher will find a way to set it all to rights and you'll have your young man back."

"My young man? Do you mean Russell?" Frances never thought of him in those terms.

"Of course. After a fair bit of time has passed his parents will see all and change their minds. You can announce your engagement and wed by the end of the Season."

That gave Frances a reason to pause. "What if I do not wish to marry him?" Except her walking speed increased. "What if I don't want an engagement?" She strode faster with each question. "What if I don't want Russell?"

Saunders grabbed hold of Frances' arm. "Please—would you slow. I can't keep up. I'm an old woman, you know."

"Sorry." How could Frances have no regard for her maid-companion? Perhaps she was wrong thinking that she and Saunders were close to the same age.

"How could you not wish to marry Sir Russell? Haven't you been writing to one another for close to a year now? You'd arranged to meet in London and planned to marry after spending the Season together."

"We had discussed it," Frances confirmed. She took Saunders by the hand, pulling it through hers so as not to lose her again. "After all that has happened...I began to think that perhaps it's all for the best."

They rounded the southeast corner of the square and out from seemingly nowhere a man suddenly appeared.

The women gasped in surprise, leaping back from him.

"*Fan! Fan!* Frances! It's all right. I am so sorry. It's me, *Dolf*." He quickly spat the words. Lord Adolphus Barker eased back with his arms outstretched in front of him to demonstrate he was of no threat to the ladies.

"It's all right, Saunders." Frances realized they weren't in danger and tried to calm her maid.

"Lord Adolphus, what a fright you've given us." Saunders had clutched her throat and still had difficulty catching her breath. "What do you think you are doing?"

"I had to see Lady Frances, speak to her." He side-stepped in front of the ladies to keep them from moving away from him.

"There are proper ways of going about that and this is not it," she uttered in a disapproving tone. "Highly unacceptable behavior."

"I was afraid I'd be turned away at Langford House."

"You might well be." Saunders kept a tight hold of Frances' arm.

Despite his unconventional methods, Lord Adolphus was already here and Frances saw no harm in speaking to him.

"Do you mind, Saunders?" Frances would not deny him a few moments of her time. It was best to have this conversation over and done, suspecting this would not be pleasant.

"I don't know." A side-long glance at the distasteful intruder did not seem to pass muster by the maid's standards. "It's not proper to meet like this."

"We will be only a few steps ahead of you. That way you can observe every action and intervene if you see the need." Frances bargained on her behalf or was it for Lord Adolphus? She did not wish to make a scene in public for she did not wish people to stare.

"All right, then." Saunders, once again, allowed her charge to convince her otherwise.

"Thank you." Frances gestured to Lord Adolphus they should move forward. She made no motion to take his arm and if he thought about offering it she would decline. "What is it you wish to say?"

He cleared his throat. Did he know this would be his last chance to speak with her? Did he believe he could change her mind about *them*? "I wanted to know if you've received my flowers."

"They arrived at the house," Frances said coolly. She did not comment on their appearance nor how they made her feel. They were beautiful and made her feel horrid, reminding her of how little he truly meant to her.

"Did you like them?" Was that hope in his voice?

"Lady Langford thought they were unexceptional and a flagrant waste of money."

"I just wanted to say how sorry I was—am. I've made an

enormous mistake. I should have applied for a license and wed you as soon as possible."

"As *soon as possible* after our engagement? Or after the first or second time you delayed our wedding?" There was no right answer. He could never explain to Frances' or her parents' satisfaction.

"I am sorry. I should have— We should have—" Desperation laced his words.

"We did not." And nothing would change that nor how her feelings for him had altered. "What is it you want, sir?"

With the inability to take hold of her hand he clasped his own together. "I want a second chance," he emoted.

"*Second?* Don't you mean fourth? Or perhaps it is *fifth.*" When he said nothing she continued, "Would you care for me to enumerate the various reasons you've listed as to why we should not marry?"

"Frances...*Fan,* I promise this time will be—" He sounded desperate and pleaded with her.

"I'm sorry, your lordship, there will not be *another* chance for you." Frances would not allow herself to be treated in this manner. How much need she endure before it became too much? She had reached her limit with Lord Adolphus and her answer would have to be No.

"But you cared for me, I know you did." He tried to plead with her.

"Yes, perhaps at one time I did. Over the past two years, you have ruined any amiable feelings I may have harbored and have now made it impossible to think of you with any kindness." Frances was only being honest with him. He had had his chance and she had moved on.

"I'm sorry you feel that way," he said rather unsympathetically.

"It is rather a shame. Good day to you, sir." She turned her head to speak over her shoulder. "Shall we go home now, Saunders?"

The maid paused for Frances to move back a few steps to join her. The two left Lord Adolphus in the park, crossed the street, and headed home, down South Audley Street.

"SIR CHRISTOPHER WILL ARRIVE AT NINE TO COLLECT YOU AND Saunders for this evening's party." Lady Langford informed her daughter upon her return home.

"*Sir Christopher*? Sir Christopher Glory?" Frances felt a bit confused. "The very same Sir Christopher Glory who dueled for my cousin Victoria's honor? The very same man whose actions caused my engagement to Sir Russell Crawford to be canceled?"

Saunders pulled off her bonnet and listened with interest.

"Yes, dear, the very same," her mother confirmed. "And Saunders, you will be chaperone."

"And I am to be seen with him, on his arm, at a Society party?" Frances wondered exactly what had been agreed upon by her cousin and her mother.

"Yes, dear. Exactly." Lady Langford looked to be the model of calm. "It is in hopes that your reputation will not only be repaired but perhaps improved by appearing with him."

Frances turned to Saunders and murmured, "Has the world gone mad?"

"When you find out, let me know. If I am going out this evening I'd best prepare. I'm not young anymore and it takes me more time." Saunders headed for the staircase and climbed the stairs.

"Come in and I shall tell you of his visit." Lady Langford led the way to her sitting room. They interrupted a passing maid busy with her duties. "Will you have tea sent in?"

"At once, ma'am." The servant bobbed a curtsy and saw immediately to her ladyship's request.

"Mama, I am not acquainted with Sir Christopher." Frances had seen him yesterday, if only for a moment. And they were related, in a loose way. Her cousin was his half-sister. Still...how could Frances' own mother allow her to attend a ball with a man who was no better than a stranger?

"Sir Christopher is your *cousin*, dear. That cannot be disputed." Lady Langford was very insistent. "The duel has made him celebrated and quite fashionable."

"*Fashionable?* As in a style of hat or color of gown?" Frances really had never heard anything more ridiculous.

"People are emulating him. They think him most heroic." Lady Langford sat in her favorite chair.

"And being seen in his company is to repair my reputation?" Frances lowered herself onto the chair closest to her mother.

"If it is to be revived, he is the one to accomplish it. And if all goes well you may meet someone new—"

"*Someone new?*" Frances interrupted. "Then you do not expect me to renew my acquaintance with Sir Russell?"

"Even if you do still care for him, dear. I'm afraid that Lord and Lady Emerson would not look upon you as a favorable match. I am terribly sorry." Lady Langford's smile faded.

"Not to worry, Mama, I did not have my heart set on him, in any case." And if there was someone out there for her, she would be the luckiest earl's daughter in the world.

"That is good to hear. All I ask is that you make the most of this chance."

"Which may be my last," Frances added.

"Which *could* very well be your last, and do make something of it." Lady Langford took hold of Frances' hand and gave it a small squeeze. "You have been very unlucky in love but perhaps this time you will succeed."

"I will do my best, Mama." Frances forced a smile to reassure her mother but it did nothing to comfort her.

"That is good to hear, dear. It is all I can ask, and your father will be most pleased."

The tea tray arrived and right behind her was a footman with a salver. The tray was placed on the table at Lady Langford's elbow and the footman lowered the salver, offering its contents to Frances.

Me? She retrieved the note at the very same time her mother asked, "Who is that from?"

The handwriting was immediately known to her. *Russell.* And she wondered what he wanted.

"Do you intend to keep this private?" Sounding uninterested, her mother busied herself with pouring tea.

"Of course not." Frances had paused at seeing Russell's handwriting for the same reason she had startled upon seeing Adolphus earlier. Both had been unexpected. She broke the seal and unfolded the letter to read:

Dearest,

 I plan to attend the Alton-Smith ball this evening. I sincerely hope that you will as well.

 Yrs, Russell

"He will be attending the Alton-Smith ball and would like to meet me there." Frances paraphrased for her mother.

"We do not know the specifics of your evening as of yet. It will be up to Sir Christopher to choose the venue," Lady Langford began. "If, however, you should attend the same party, it would be a waste of your time to spend any of it with Sir Russell."

"Agreed." But Frances wasn't sure how she could avoid him if it were to come about. Perhaps having Sir Christopher at her side would come in handy.

"Let's have some tea, dear, and discuss what you should wear tonight." Lady Langford held out a cup for her daughter.

Frances folded Russell's letter and pushed it to one side, away from her mother and out of her mind.

fourteen

GREETINGS AND INTRODUCTIONS WERE made to all the members of Sir Christopher's party who rode in his carriage: Lady Frances, her chaperone Mrs. Saunders, and Albert Winslow, with varying levels of nervousness and hopes.

Christopher had high expectations of success for Lord and Lady Alton-Smith's party. During the drive, he made the suggestion, "If all goes well tonight, perhaps we should consider attending the Venetian Breakfast tomorrow morning together."

"As you wish, sir," Lady Frances replied without a show of enthusiasm.

She had every right to remain reserved about what *might* happen. It may have been a bit soon to speak about further commitments when they did not know the outcome of this evening.

"Unless there is some other gentleman who wishes to escort you?" he suggested in a hopeful manner. Lady Langford would be very happy to see her daughter on the arm of some new prospect.

Lady Frances glanced up at him and she remained silent.

The coach stopped, there was a collective deep breath. They all readied themselves for what lay ahead. Christopher entered the grand residence with Lady Frances on his arm, Mrs. Saunders, and Albee followed. There were many people in attendance and the volume of the conversation grew the farther they moved inside.

"You are collecting some notice," Albee said to Christopher.

"I can see that." Christopher was quite adamant that the point of this evening was solely for Lady Frances' benefit, not his. He would do what he could to put his cousin forward. He secured her small hand in the crook of his arm, preventing them from being separated.

Sir Christopher seemed to attract quite a bit of attention from what she could tell. His steady hold of her hand assured her he had no intention of allowing her to slip away and that gave her added confidence.

"Mr. Morris. Lord Walton." Mr. Winslow inclined his head to each as they entered the residence. Frances did not know if these gentlemen had previously known him before he had come to Town. "Sir Roland. Lord Harrison."

Sir Christopher made occasional acknowledgments to various other guests while he resettled her hand on his arm. His touch was firm and comforting. She tilted her head, raised her chin, and gazed into the room to see what she had to...what she must confront. Nothing, no one, to fear. She then looked about her, searching for a familiar face. Hoping there would be one, knowing, most probably, one would not be found. It had been two years since she'd entered a London ballroom.

This experience was not unlike that of her first Season. *Unlike* her first Season, she was not a naive young girl but older, and she hoped wiser. That is what two failed engagements had done for her. It was an education one did not find in a schoolroom. This time, she felt less unsure and more confident in herself.

Those who had accompanied her this evening, although distantly related, were strangers. Frances need not fear the stares from the gentlemen guests directed her way, their attention centered on Sir Christopher, or rather upon his waistcoat.

A glance toward his garment would have been difficult for any passers-by to ignore. He had drawn one side of his coat to display. It was a high-necked affair with deep pink and red, large-petalled flowers, and vibrant green curling vines around a shiny golden trellised background. The garment made quite a statement and mesmerized Frances for a few minutes, she had never seen anything quite its like before.

Was it a new London fashion?

Soon she realized that one by one, the gentlemen around them were shifting their gazes to her, the lady on Sir Christopher's arm.

"What is that, Walton?" Sir Christopher stared pointedly into the crowd.

"*An introduction?*" Walton's succinct answer held a bit of impatience. "If you would be so kind."

"Let it be known that my lady has already promised me the first dance and our fellow companion, Mr. Winslow, the second Country Dance."

"Wouldn't want to step on your toes, *Glory*!" another one of the onlookers remarked then others guffawed.

"I will inquire if my lady would care for introductions to the likes of you all." He gestured to those standing before him. "I make it clear that I recommend none of you. It is dependent upon the young lady to make that decision for herself." Sir Christopher held his hand up to halt the growing grumblings of the onlookers. "What is that you say, *Cousin*?" He tilted his head as if paying rapt attention to her whisper. "No, I shan't allow you to dance with any disreputable scapegraces."

"Oh, Sir Christopher!" Frances made a small gasp and slapped his arm. "I said nothing of the kind!" The gentleman chuckled at her reaction. She could feel her cheeks warm, partially from the teasing itself and partially from the attention it drew to her.

This was followed by introduction after introduction of gentlemen, a continual stream of *How do you dos*, and requests for a dance. It did not take long for her dance card to fill and the introductions continued. As good as Frances was with recalling names and faces, the sheer number of Sir Christopher's acquaintances put her memory to the test.

The start of the first dance saved her from further introductions and Sir Christopher escorted her to the dance floor.

"I think that went rather well," Sir Christopher commented in a rather elevated tone. He seemed quite pleased with himself and ran his hand down his waistcoat.

"*I* think those gentlemen might have been more interested in currying favor with you" —or at least his tailor— "than winning my good opinion."

"What?" He turned toward her sharply, allowing his jacket to fall back into place. "That wasn't my intention at all."

Frances met his eyes only for an instant before pulling her gaze from him, facing forward, preparing for the dance. Perhaps she was wrong but that's how it had appeared to her. The music started. Frances and Sir Christopher began to dance.

Since Frances' dance card was full, she spent a great deal of time occupied—on her feet, on the dance floor. Again, she had the feeling her partner, whoever he should be *this* time, was not as interested in her as Sir Christopher. The telltale sign was the glances past her toward the baronet who stood to one side and wore an expression of approval.

During one of the dances, Frances could not recall which, where the lines were moving, the participants passed one another, and she saw—*Emmeline!* She and Frances both gasped when setting eyes on the other.

"I'll find you," Lady Emmeline mouthed. Frances nodded, feeling the most elated she had since her arrival and her mood lightened immensely.

The remainder of the dance, which seemed to stretch on for far longer than what was realistic, was finally over.

"Thank you, Lord Walton." Frances tried to sound gracious but could not wish him away soon enough.

"It was my pleasure, Lady Frances." Lord Walton smiled, bowed, and moved on seamlessly from her to Sir Christopher. The two men engaged in such a compelling conversation that had not even been attempted with her.

It was of no matter. Frances ignored the two and glanced about for Lady Emmeline. *There she was.*

Lady Emmeline brightened when she spotted Frances and waved to gain her attention. She motioned to her *cortege*, there must have been five or six of them, to remain behind as she progressed toward Frances alone. My goodness, she was popular.

"Lady Emmeline, how good it is to see you. I was beginning to think I didn't know a soul. I had no idea you were to attend this evening." It was very good to see a familiar face. It seemed to Frances that Lady Emmeline knew a great many people. Not *everyone*, Frances realized. Lady Emmeline's attention began to drift off to her right, to Sir Christopher, who stood behind Frances.

"Are you acquainted with Sir Christopher—and his friend

Mr. Winslow?" Frances thought a glimmer sparked in Lady Emmeline's eyes at the mention of the baronet's name.

"Sir Christopher? Miss Stiles' brother? No, I have not had the pleasure of an introduction," Lady Emmeline replied, her smile widened. "Since my acquaintance to Pauline and Miss Stiles, I feel as if I half know him already."

"Then you will allow me to amend this situation. Give me a moment, will you?" Frances pivoted, reaching her gloved hand out to her *cousin*, placing it lightly on his sleeve.

She gained his attention at her touch. He glanced at her face and halted his current conversation at once, excusing himself with a nod.

"What is it, my dear?" He stepped toward Frances, all his attention focused upon her.

"I wish to make you known to an acquaintance your sister and I met at the Chandlers'."

"I would be delighted. Allow me to...." His attention swiveled momentarily away from her. "*Albee*, join me if you would." Mr. Winslow returned to Sir Christopher's side and they stepped closer to the two young ladies.

Sir Christopher's expression altered once he gazed upon Lady Emmeline before Frances could make the introductions.

At her beauty, no doubt. Frances could not blame him. He was, after all, only a man.

"Lady Emmeline, may I introduce Sir Christopher Glory and his friend Mr. Winslow?" It was then Frances noticed what could only be described as *an aura* enveloping Lady Emmeline when she shifted her attention to Sir Christopher. Her eyes brightened, the gold streaks in her hair seemed to shimmer, it must have been apparent to those standing close.

Both gentlemen murmured, "How do you do," and bowed. Mr. Winslow made a gracious leg but Sir Christopher's effort was quite elaborate. He fully extended his arms in a grand sweep and descended low. Frances' *cousin* wished to make an impression.

"How do you do?" Lady Emmeline replied. "Sir Christopher, Mr. Winslow." But it was obvious she was quite taken with the baronet. There was a slight smile and a barest hint of a dimple on her cheek.

Frances glanced from Sir Christopher to Lady Emmeline and back again before it was obvious *the aura* was meant for the baronet and not his friend. It appeared to Frances that Mr. Winslow was unaffected. Sir Christopher, it seemed, was completely bewitched.

The two neared and it was quite apparent they had eyes only for the other...those around them must have faded from sight.

"May I be so bold as to ask if you happen to have a dance available?"

"I'm afraid not for the next several sets," Lady Emmeline relayed the disappointing news, her voice tinged with a bit of sadness. "I have, however, retained my supper dance...for some particular gentleman...should I meet him." Her radiant smile was meant only for him but there was no hiding such a treasure for anyone to see.

"Then I shall claim your supper dance and remain patient until then." He lifted her gloved hand to his lips.

"Excuse me, Lady Frances," Mr. Winslow said softly to her. "Our country dance is soon to begin but I must first have a word with Sir Christopher."

"Of course," she replied. The instant Mr. Winslow had turned his back to address Sir Christopher, Frances noticed someone approaching her from the opposite side.

"*Fan,* dearest," was the low, soft whisper to gain her attention. It was Sir Russell Crawford.

"Russell?" She knew he was to attend but she never thought him so bold as to approach her. While Mr. Winslow and Sir Christopher were nearby, their backs were turned to her, unable to see the young man approach.

"You look lovely." Russell gazed at her, only her. He did not seem concerned that they may be interrupted for Mr. Winslow would return at any moment.

"Thank you," she said out of the habit of politeness. Frances felt uncomfortable with his abrupt appearance. Being seen together in public, she realized, would be unacceptable to his family.

"I wish to let you know that my parents are...reconsidering our engagement. They do not fully realize that...not at this moment but...." He paused, reaching to take hold of her gloved hand. Frances realized the simple gesture displayed a false intimacy. "Rest assured, they will change their opinion regarding our marriage. I do hope it will not be too long until we can resume our courtship."

The gentle smile that graced his lips reminded her of the young man she remembered two years ago. They'd first met at a party much like this and he spoke softly to her as he did now. Was it his quiet manner that made him less desirable than the persistent Lord Adolphus?

"Will you attend the Venetian Breakfast at Lady Chesney's tomorrow morning?"

"Yes, I am planning to meet a few others there." Frances recalled Sir Christopher speak of the event.

"Would you do me the honor of escorting you?" The anguish in his eyes.... "I won't stay. I wouldn't want to disrupt your plans."

His affection seemed to remain consistent throughout their association. Frances doubted herself. Perhaps she had forgotten how it had been between them. It was, after all, two years ago.

He was the one who had suggested they meet again and before declaring they marry but there was an understanding between them. They would wait until they came to Town, met again, and then final decisions would be made.

To accept Russell's minor request...it seemed such a little thing.... Why did she hesitate?

"I don't know." How would Frances explain this to her mother? What would she say to Sir Christopher who carefully staged this reentry into Society for her?

"It is just a drive in my phaeton to Lady Chesney's. It is only for a bit of time to be alone together. We have not yet had a chance to be truly private." His voice—so warm and encouraging. His tone—so very soft. How could she say No?

Frances believed giving him false hope would not be in the best interest for either of them. Perhaps if she took that time, time alone with him, and explained that despite his parents' objections that they may also conclude a match between them would not happen. She was certain he would understand...far better than Lord Adolphus had.

"Very well." Frances decided. She was not sure how she would explain herself to Sir Christopher or her mother but would come up with something. "I shall tell my party I will meet them there."

"Thank you, *Fan*." Russell smiled.

"I certainly hope Lord Adolphus does not make an appearance." Why she said such a thing....

"*Adolphus*? He is in Town *now*? Is he *here*?" Russell's expression changed. He glanced around in what Frances thought an agitated manner.

"He made his presence known to me this afternoon and I cannot say I was pleased to see him."

"*Damn* him—" He gasped, shocking himself at his lack of

control. "I beg your pardon, my dearest *Fan*. How dare that cur bother you!"

Frances had never before seen the type of flare that sparked in Russell's eyes.

"If it were up to me.... It is of no matter now," Russell murmured and gazed at Frances, once again smiling and bowing over her hand. "I shall call for you in the morning, shall I?"

"Yes, thank you." She returned his civility and realized that he could be quite charming. "I think it best you do not come into the house. I shall keep watch for your arrival myself."

"Very well. Until tomorrow, then." He released her hand and stepped back from her just as Mr. Winslow returned to Frances' side.

"I beg your pardon, Lady Frances. I did not wish to leave you standing alone." Mr. Winslow addressed her as if completely unaware with whom she had been keeping company.

"Not at all, sir." The mere omission of those few moments felt as if she were being dishonest. It certainly felt as if there was some dishonesty on her part.

"Shall we make our way to the ballroom?" He offered her his arm.

"I...." She looked up at him through her dark brown lashes from her downcast eyes. "Would you be terribly disappointed if we did not dance?"

"Well...I mean.... If you do not wish—" He could not restrain an audible sigh of relief. "Thank goodness."

"Whyever do you say that?" She sounded somewhat alarmed at his reaction.

It had nothing to do with her. "It is nothing personal, I can assure you." Albert's reasons had to do with him alone. "I cannot tell you how long it's been since I've danced. I'm rather afraid I might irreparably harm you...your toes."

She smiled and seemed relieved at the reprieve. "I have danced every set. I cannot tell you how fatigued.... I want more than just a moment to catch my breath."

"It matters not what your reason. I must confess, I am grateful." Albert chuckled, feeling a bit nervous. He had no wish to offend her. "Would you care to take a stroll about the room? Perhaps we can find some fresh air."

"I think that is worth a try." She addressed him sincerely then looked away to take in the room and the crowd surrounding them. "It is quite the crush."

Could it be she was just as uncomfortable as he was in such situations? Albert took a moment to regard her before offering his arm.

"Thank you." She laid her hand upon his sleeve, looked up at him, and smiled.

Albert found Lady Frances quite agreeable, pretty. Different from Lady Emmeline, Frances may not have had the captivating beauty that immediately attracted a man upon introduction. She had an admirable maturity that, to him, seemed far preferable for a sensible man: good sense and an even temperament. He didn't care for a virago who was led by whims and silly notions. What man would?

"I believe Lady Emmeline has quite enchanted Kit." Albert led Lady Frances past the dance floor where they spied Kit observing...admiring Lady Emmeline as she graced the dance floor with her current partner. *The poor fellow*. Although dancing with said lady in a quadrille, he had not held her attention. It was, by Albert's estimation, focused toward the side-lines, on his friend.

"Do you not find Lady Emmeline agreeable?" Lady Frances sounded curious.

Albert considered himself quite immune to Lady Emmeline's charms and he wondered if it was obvious. He glanced at the dance floor, at Lady Emmeline. "She is beautiful but...I must admit what she has may be only beauty."

"Oh, no. She is truly very accomplished." Lady Frances stilled, bringing Albert to a standstill.

"That may well be, *Cousin*, but I am not about to take the time to make the discovery. I did not come to London to find a wife," he replied.

"I see." His companion's gloved hand resting upon his sleeve shifted. His relaxed attitude made her feel quite at ease. Frances faced forward, smiled, and moved on again.

RUSSELL LEFT HIS FRANCES AND RACED THROUGH THE BALLROOM to make his way to the card room. If he attended, that was where he would find Adolphus Barker. The scoundrel was not only interested in the ladies but he liked to play cards and dice. Only females with money...large dowries drew this younger son's interest.

Russell stepped through the doors and scanned the room for Barker, coming up empty-handed. Perhaps he did not attend, perhaps.... Russell strode to the refreshment room. There, standing next to the table, was Adolphus. The sight of him enraged Russell. By God, he would teach the cad a lesson. He might plant him a facer right there if he, in any way, dared disparage *his* Frances.

"A word alone, sir, if you please." Russell ground out through his gritted teeth.

"Crawford? Fancy seeing you here. It's been a long time," a slightly inebriated Adolphus remarked.

"I warn you, do not make a nuisance of yourself to Frances."

"A *nuisance?* Me?" Barker seemed surprised at the notion.

"Nor should you cause a spectacle for Lord and Lady Langford. They have been through enough on your behalf."

"My behalf?" Again the claim baffled him. "I'll tell you, Frances was more than delighted to see me."

Russell felt his ire rise within him. It was all he could do to keep from shouting. "If you do not step outside with me now I shall see you on the field in the morning."

There were several howls, taunting the two adversaries, followed by low murmurs.

"And what exactly are we to meet over?"

"A certain lady who no longer wishes you to inflict your intentions upon her. You have had your chance and now you must step aside."

"Ah...she is to remain nameless, is she?" Barker chuckled.

"Do not dare utter her name lest you wish me to strangle you here and now."

Nervous laughter ensued. They could not know if Russell was serious or merely voicing a threat. It was *not* a threat.

"Tomorrow? Why so soon?" Barker was not taking this seriously.

Russell leaned close, lowered the volume of his voice, and willed himself not to shout. "Because I cannot bear the thought of you drawing another breath. Your existence causes me such distress…. I want it to end." He moved back slowly to regard the expression on the face before him.

Quiet terror shone in Barker's eyes. He was frightened, and he should have been because Russell had every intention of killing him.

"I leave for home now. Send the details at once, lest you be branded a coward." With that, Russell left.

fifteen

CHALK FARM

"Seven! Eight! Nine! Ten!"

After taking their agreed upon twenty paces, Sir Russell Crawford turned to face his opponent.

He had folded his coat lapels across his chest, masking the front of the white of his shirt as not to provide an obvious target. His hat was firmly wedged on his head and he stood side-on toward his opponent, making himself as narrow as possible.

Russell straightened his arm, aiming at Barker, and did not hesitate to fire. He would dispatch the cad at the earliest moment, eliminating his competition, and ending a wretched blight placed upon this Earth.

The pistol in Lord Adolphus Barker's hand visibly shook. He was reputed to be *a fair shot*—which would not be good enough pitted against Russell. He would need a great deal of luck on this day.

After waiting for these last two years, Russell would be free to make Lady Frances *his* wife.

He pulled the trigger a fraction of a second before two booms, sounding near-simultaneously, filled the air. A cloud of smoke engulfed the two men momentarily before Barker fell to the ground.

Mr. Braithwaite, the surgeon, ran to the wounded man's side followed by the seconds. Barker, as suspected, had merely missed his target proving he was less than a fair shot and luck had not been with him. The scoundrel had not meant to delope and had taken the duel as seriously as Russell.

"We're done and I have won!" Russell announced to all in attendance. With no regard to the condition of his opponent, he walked off the field, handing his pistol to Harriot. "Wish me well," he said to James before stepping up into the box of his phaeton. Taking the ribbons and releasing the brake, Russell called to his cattle and was off to South Audley Street.

RUSSELL HALTED HIS PHAETON IN FRONT OF THE LANGFORD residence and stopped short of stepping onto the walk. As Lady Frances had requested, he waited outside, feeling perhaps a bit too impatient. She was not one to be late. Now if collecting her would go just as smoothly as removing Barker, Russell surmised there would be no problem.

The front door opened and his heart began to pound at the sight of Frances. Dressed predominantly in pale yellow, she reminded Russell of a primrose, the very loveliest, in a field of flowers.

In his excitement, Russell met her halfway down the walk, holding out his hand to steady her. "Shall we be off?"

"Mama says she will meet me within the hour." She told him and accepted his aid stepping up into the phaeton.

"Did you mention that I would see you delivered?" For anyone to know the details of this morning's plans might make accomplishing his more difficult. Hopping up and taking the driver's seat, Russell picked up the ribbons, whip, and released the brake.

"Uh...I'm afraid I was a bit vague on that." She carefully laid her parasol across her lap and placed her reticule on top.

"That probably is best," Russell replied. Actually, he thought that was perfect. "Hold on, *dearest*." He warned and sprang the horses.

"*Goodness!*" Frances cried. She grasped her items on her lap with the sudden jolt. The first few minutes were spent in silence and she sat wide-eyed. There was the rush of the scenery, the wind, and the noise of the wheels for one to overcome when unaccustomed to the speed.

"Russell," Frances began. "I wonder if I might speak to you about something...serious."

"Of course, *Fan*." Although he was busy with the horses, his full attention need not be on them entirely. "I'm listening."

"I understand that we have spent many months writing to one another."

"That has been wonderful." He had written, many times, how their *friendship* meant everything to him.

"Our correspondence meant the world to me...at the time." She could only speak when the ruts and bumps in the road allowed for conversation. "When your letters came over the last year, it was a time when I was very vulnerable."

The phaeton slowed to nearly a stop as cross-traffic passed in both directions before them. He cracked the whip in the air, urging his team up to speed.

"Many years ago...when we first met, you know that I had been courting Lord Adolphus."

"Yes, and you chose him over me." He turned his head toward her and smiled. He would not hold that decision against her. Russell put that unfortunate situation behind him. It was poor timing on his part. Had he met her sooner, had he acted.... None of that mattered anymore.

"I know now my involvement with him was a mistake."

"He is not worthy of you."

"It's only tha—OH!" The phaeton made a sudden stop catching Frances unprepared.

"Sorry." Russell apologized. "Are you all right?" After checking on her well-being, he cracked his whip to urge his cattle moving again.

"I'm afraid I must be frank on the matter and tell you that my marital choices do not lie between the two of you. I think— I think—" Frances looked around.

Had she noticed they had not passed any of the landmarks she might know? Or that they did not travel down Regent Street? Had she noticed the city surroundings being replaced by rural landscape?

Russell wondered if she realized that they were not heading to the Venetian Breakfast. Instead, he had taken a different direction and was heading out of London.

ALBERT HAD ARRIVED AT THE ARLINGTON STREET RESIDENCE WITH Kit. If he were to be honest, Albert looked forward to seeing Lady Frances again after spending time with her last night. A leisurely stroll outdoors amongst the foliage and flowers with her would be delightful, far better than a turn in a crowded indoor ballroom.

"Dear me, Sir Christopher, thank goodness you are here."

Lady Langford appeared to be agitated, breathless, and quite beside herself.

"What is it, my lady?" Kit threw a warning glance at his friend. It appeared they both understood something extraordinary had happened to cause the countess distress.

"Where is Lady Frances, may I ask?" Albert could not wait for her to voice her thoughts.

"Is she not with you? I had thought.... I had hoped...." Lady Langford extricated her handkerchief from the wrist of her sleeve and pressed it to her eyes. "I was to meet her here and.... I am afraid that she is not to be found."

"Not to be found? Are you certain?" Kit replied, understandably, in alarm. "Did you not arrive together?"

"No. I thought you were.... I suppose.... Well, she did not say who she was to travel with exactly." Her ladyship pressed the handkerchief to her eyes. "She left early, perhaps an hour ago. She told us she would meet us here. I had thought she traveled with you."

"No." Kit glanced at Albert. Her ladyship's anxiety had spread to both men. "She did not."

Lady Frances' chaperone Mrs. Saunders came upon the small group and reported, "There is still no sign of her, my lady."

"Where can she be? She must be here—she must!" Lady Langford was distraught and on the verge of becoming very emotional. "Sir Christopher, what are we to do?"

"I suggest you and Mrs. Saunders return home and inquire as to who called for Lady Frances this morning." Kit pulled her arm through his and escorted her to where some of the coaches waited.

Albert followed with the chaperone trying to keep the older lady from lagging. Because of the emergency, Kit managed to commandeer someone else's transport. Albert handed Mrs. Saunders up the steps followed by Lady Langford.

"Please send word to Grayson House once you discover the answer," Kit told her. "Jane will know how to contact me."

"But what if Frances.... If she's— she's—" Lady Langford continued to speak to him through the opened window.

"Mr. Winslow and I will make a thorough search. If she is here, we will find her. If not" —They would have to see what needed to be done in that circumstance— "You shall hear from me."

The carriage moved off. The two men returned to where they had met Lady Langford.

"I find this very worrying, Kit."

"So do I. Let us begin our search." Kit signaled in which direction he would start and in what direction Albert should head. "Let's see if we can find some answers, shall we?"

"We'll meet back in say...a half hour?"

"Done." Both men went their designated ways. Each kept their eyes open for Lady Frances. They spoke to people who might have seen her if she had indeed arrived at all. But no one had. There were some men, who gossiped about a duel taking place early that morning, and they spoke of the argument that precipitated the meeting on the field the night before. Lady Frances' name had been mentioned.

A half hour later they returned to the meeting point. They ran once they caught sight of one another.

"We need to return to Grayson House." Kit clapped Albert on the shoulder, indicating that they should depart. The carriage had already been called for and waited in the designated area.

"Did you hear about the duel this morning?" Kit said between his long, deliberate steps.

"Sir Russell Crawford and Lord Adolphus Barker?" Albert had been told, while keeping apace with his friend.

"Barker escaped with his life and there were whispers of a flight to Gretna Green." Kit opened the door and motioned for Albert to enter first.

"Not by Lord Adolphus, I trust."

"No. I think that highly unlikely." Kit entered the transport, closed the door, and rapped on the roof.

The coach surged off.

sixteen

CHRISTOPHER AND ALBEE USED the time during the drive home to discuss the possible scenarios with which they might be faced, none of the outcomes were favorable. There was no time to lose with Lady Frances' abduction, her rescue must be immediate.

"Horses will be faster," Christopher explained what he had in mind. "We'll have the best chance to intercept them."

"Agreed," Albee replied. Christopher was glad to have his friend by his side during this undertaking.

"I must see to my responsibilities," Christopher spoke out loud, compiling a list of items to be done. "I'll send Jane to stay with Pauline. I'm sending Mrs. Heffelfinger and my coach to collect Mrs. Saunders. They will follow us until we catch up to Crawford and Lady Frances and care for her after we find her."

It was not a question of *if*, it was *when*. He and Albee would find Lady Frances and see that she was safely returned to her parents.

"How will we know how he will proceed to Gretna?" Albee, who had spent a good deal of his young adult life secluded on his estate in Somerset, wanted to know.

The coach rolled to a stop in front of Grayson House. "I imagine he will take the most common route—the Great North Road," Christopher answered before opening the door and hopping out.

Preparations for horses, traveling coach, and their personal effects were left up to Albee. Straightaway he directed a stable hand to call upon the residence of Lord Emerson for a description of the missing vehicle as to identify Sir Russell's transport while Kit went directly to his library to draft various missives, making other arrangements.

Christopher called for Mrs. Heffelfinger just as he sat to write one of many missives. His first was to Lady Frances' parents.

Lord and Lady Langford,

I apologize for not presenting this news in person but I fear there is no time to spare. I do not wish to alarm you but I believe that Lady Frances has been abducted by Sir Russell Crawford. His destination —Gretna Green for an elopement. You must remember that he cares for her—I do not believe her life is in danger while she remains in his company.

Albert Winslow and I plan to ride within the hour to pursue the two in hopes of catching the couple long before they reach the border. I shall keep you informed as to our progress.

I have provided a traveling coach for my aunt Mrs. Heffelfinger to collect Lady Frances' maid to follow us. When the rescue of your daughter has been accomplished, the ladies will be nearby to lend aid and see to her care until she is returned home.

Wish us luck. Yr Servant,

Sir Christopher Glory

Christopher sent off the footman with his letter just as Mrs. Heffelfinger entered.

"I came at once, Sir Christopher. What is it you need?"

"Will you be seated, Mrs. H?" There was still so much to be done and he needed her to follow his instructions, sparing him a fit of the vapors, swooning, or a surplus of female emotions that might delay his departure.

She somehow sensed the importance of the situation and the wringing of her handkerchief began when she lowered slowly onto a chair.

"A crisis has befallen *our* family, Mrs. H, and we must all act together to see to its favorable resolution."

"Dear *God*, what has happened?" Her hands stilled and rested on her lap as she paid close attention.

"I need to depend on you. I expect what I ask may be very difficult, indeed."

"Gracious!" The color drained from her face and he hoped she would show the good sense and maturity he knew she possessed.

"Now is not the time to be missish."

"No." Her voice sounded hollow but resolute. "I am quite able to do anything you require, sir."

"Good." Christopher went on to explain. "The traveling coach is preparing to leave in an hour's time."

He instructed that she needed to pack for her and Jane, enough for several days, and escort Jane to the Chandler residence to be placed under Mrs. Chandler's care. Mrs. Heffelfinger and the coach would then continue to the Langford residence and take on Mrs. Saunders. The two would progress up the Great North Road following behind him and Albee's pursuit of Lady Frances.

"Do not say so—Lady Frances? A runaway marriage? I

would not have thought it." The news shocked Mrs. Heffelfinger. "With whom?"

"Sir Russell Crawford. I must inform you that I do not believe she has gone of her own accord."

Mrs. Heffelfinger's second gasp, accompanied by tears welling in her eyes. "No!"

"When we find her, and we shall," he said with assurance, "You and Mrs. Saunders will be most appreciated and of great comfort to her, I am sure."

By her reaction, he could see she understood the possible danger involved, what had been asked of her, and what she might endure during the recovery of the earl's daughter and subsequent safe return to her family.

"I have already sent messages to Mrs. Chandler and Lord Langford, both should be expecting you."

Mrs. Heffelfinger pressed her lips together in an attempt to suppress her overwrought nerves. She was to be commended. The woman was trying her best and a muffled sob was all Christopher heard.

"If you will excuse me, Sir Christopher." She stood with a seemingly renewed composure. "I will see to our preparations at once."

"Thank you, Mrs. H." Christopher drew in a deep breath. It was with some apprehension that he composed his final letter.

Dear Martin,

I know you are still nursing a wound and would rather be left alone. I do not wish to burden you but I need a great favor, my friend.

I ask that you fulfill my social commitments for the next several days. I understand that you and this young lady are already acquainted thus making my request an easier one for me.

I was to escort Lady Emmeline Cordia-Darling this morning at the Venetian Breakfast, meeting her at Lady Chesney's residence on Arlington Street. I realize the party is currently in progress but rest assured that if you leave now you will still arrive before her.

I have also promised to take her for a drive in the Park at the fashionable hour this afternoon. My final engagement was to escort her to a ball given by Lady Charlotte Dolan this evening.

I do not have time to explain my reasons at this moment. Jane, who will be under the care of Mrs. Chandler during my absence, will be residing in your house for several days and may be able to answer some of your questions as details are currently being discovered.

Yrs, Christopher

After sanding, folding, and sealing the missive, Christopher had a footman deliver it posthaste. He left the library to prepare for his journey. Jane met him at the back door just as he was about to leave.

"Please bring Cousin Frances home safe."

"I shall do my utmost." Some part of Christopher felt as if he were neglecting his sister but his duty to Lady Frances could not be more clear. "I needn't worry about you, shall I, Jane?"

"I will be with Pauline, her mother, and Martin," Jane reminded him unnecessarily. "I wish you and Mr. Winslow every success. Do be careful."

"We shall." Christopher leaned in for a hug and a kiss from Jane. She stepped back, resigned that he must leave.

Albee and the horses were ready and waiting. Settling in their saddles, they departed. They headed north with no other thought than to find Lady Frances and her abductor.

"Russell? Where are we going?" Frances gripped the seat rail, holding on for dear life. The moisture in her eyes was not from the speed in which they traveled, but from the fear welling up inside her. "Where are you taking me?"

"This is quite unorthodox, I admit, *Fan*." He laughed in a deranged manner. "I will tell you true. We are heading to Gretna."

"*Gretna*?" That would take days. And to be alone with him for a *day* would cause her reputation to be ruined. Frances glanced to her left, briefly contemplating throwing herself from the racing vehicle and good sense took over, dismissing such an impulsive action. "We cannot!"

"We must," he insisted.

"But why?" This was madness!

"Because I am not willing to lose you again." He lashed the whip over the horses, uring them to move faster.

"Lose me?" How could Frances have ever thought him agreeable?

"First my parents cancel our engagement, then that scoundrel Barker tries to win back your affections... We must act for ourselves."

"But this is not the way to go about it." How could Frances convince him? "You said yourself that your parents were reconsidering our match. Should we not wait for their approval?"

"I cannot wait any longer."

The carriage's wheel hit something and it jarred under her, causing Frances to cry out.

"Our marriage would be much more acceptable...to Society. We need to go about this in the right way. Isn't that what you want? It's what I want. We should not do this." She watched him for a reaction. Nothing she said seemed to make any difference. "We don't need to wait for the banns to be read, we could apply for a license.... I'm sure we could procure a Special License, our parents could surely arrange it."

Still, he focused on driving the horses and said nothing.

"Eloping would cause such a scandal for us, for both our families, Russell." Why did he not listen to reason?

"I understand what you're saying, *Fan*, but it is of no use. I have set plans into motion and I am not turning back." He glanced at her with a hardened look in his eyes. "Even for you."

seventeen

MARTIN PAUSED WHILE READING Kit's letter and gazed skyward. He scanned down the long stretch of street for an arriving carriage and heaved a heavy sigh. He slowly shook his head and returned to the missive.

I realize the party is currently in progress but rest assured that if you leave now you will still arrive before her.

Martin consulted his pocket watch yet again. How was it possible that he had received Christopher's written request, grumbled a bit, cleaned-up, dressed, and traveled to Arlington Street and still managed to arrive before Lady Emmeline?

It shouldn't have been.

I have also promised to take her for a drive in the Park at the fashionable hour this afternoon. My final commitment was to escort her to a ball given by Lady Charlotte Dolan this evening.

And *this* was to continue throughout the day? Waiting for

her? For hours on end? To be fair, it was not *actually* hours, it only *felt* as if it had been hours. He returned his timepiece to its place, folded the letter and slid it in his pocket, and paced in front of the house again. He'd lost count how many times. At this point he didn't want to know, it would just make him more angry.

Doing him a favor...a great *favor.* Martin repeated, grumbling to himself. *Kit.... Kit....* There was no possible repayment for a favor of this magnitude. This went beyond Martin's endurance. Almost...not quite. He drew in a breath to calm himself...to access that small bit of tolerance left within him. *If* Kit were not such a good friend....

Several carriages pulled up in the passenger area. Those were waiting to take on people to leave. There hadn't been one transport that he'd seen that *delivered* any guests. Then a lone crested-carriage drew up, containing occupants, and stopped.

A footman descended the box and lowered the steps before opening the door, and down stepped Lady Emmeline. Martin recognized her immediately and approached.

Instead of stepping down from the carriage, it appeared to Martin as if she somehow floated without disturbing a single curl upon her perfectly coiffed head. Dressed in a morning gown in a quite bold red with ivory embellishments, he had never quite beheld a young lady so daring with her color choice. Her brown eyes, framed by dark lashes added to the intense pigment complimenting the bloom in her cheeks and the smoothness of the skin. The illusion she created was quite striking.

"I beg your pardon, Lady Emmeline." Martin made what he thought was an impressive bow. It had been some years since they had renewed their acquaintance and she may not have recognized him.

Her large brown eyes did not meet his gaze and she quite successfully looked around him until he spoke words she could not avoid hearing and drew her attention.

"Our mothers are very good friends and we have previously met several years ago, I believe."

"Of course...you are Mr. Chandler, are you not?" It was the companion to the earl's daughter who addressed him.

"Yes, ma'am. I am." Martin smiled, relieved that the older woman acknowledged him. Lady Emmeline might have left him standing there speaking into the air. "I am a close friend of Sir Christopher Glory. He has sent me on his behalf."

The beauty turned her attention to him by meeting his gaze. "Sir Christopher, you say?" Actually, Martin thought she was scrutinizing him.

"Yes. There has been a family emergency and he has sent me in his place as an escort this morning."

"What?" There was a stomp of her foot displaying her displeasure and a softly uttered, "*Rude!*"

"I beg your pardon?" Martin was rather perplexed by this action.

"I thank you very much, Mr. Chandler, I accept your offer." Lady Emmeline turned to her chaperone. "My parasol, Mrs. Peckover."

The chaperone unfurled and opened the umbrella before handing it to her charge then faded into the background.

"There." Lady Emmeline held the canopy over her head, shielding the direct sunlight from her person. "Now, Mr. Chandler, if you would be so good as to offer me your arm."

Martin drew in a breath and did as he was asked, knowing it was going to be a very, very long day.

THERE WERE STILL SEVERAL HUNDREDS OF MILES TO TRAVEL UNTIL they reached the border. Frances had stopped talking, begging, pleading with Russell to reconsider after so many hours had passed. There was little use in trying to dissuade him while he was so intent on his single-minded purpose.

She was tired. Her willpower and her spirit.

Unfortunately, there was much daylight ahead of them. He only stopped for fresh horses, they could not go on forever. When they arrived at the coaching inn, a quick change of horses and a few comforts were offered before they continue on their way.

With a surreptitious glance, she met with downcast eyes from those who would not ask questions nor offer her any assistance when Frances had the impression they were fully aware of her sad circumstance. It must have been obvious that she was not a willing participant but no one seemed to care enough to intervene. This, as Russell had briefly mentioned, had been part of the 'plans he had set into motion.'

He handed Frances up to the seat, seemingly with great care and concern for her. If he had any true regard for her, he would have turned back to London. He had previously secured her parasol behind them to keep it out of the way. She settle in her uncomfortable seat, held onto the reticule resting in her lap, and with her other hand, curled her fingers tight around the seat rail, preparing to take flight.

The phaeton flew across the dirt road with all its bumps and holes toward Scotland. Russell's energy seemed boundless and he urged the horses forward, cracking the whip over their heads when the speed diminished. The endless rounds of changing horses and death-defying travel would continue as long as there was daylight.

And there were many, many more hours until the sun set. Then Frances had to endure the final day's stop and face the night ahead, alone with Russell.

"WHAT DO YOU THINK THEY'RE DOING NOW, JANE?" PAULINE SAT with her friend in the sitting room with the mending basket between them. Her hands were busy but her idle mind could not refrain from speculating regarding Lady Frances' drama.

"Who?" Jane replied. "Kit and Mr. Winslow or Cousin Frances and Sir Russell?"

Either choice was worth discussing. Up until a fortnight ago, duels, runaway marriages, and daring rescues did not happen to people she knew.

"All of them," Pauline retorted, sounding a bit abrupt. "Here we sit doing nothing while Sir Christopher and Mr. Winslow race up the Great North Road to find Lady Frances and Sir Russell."

"Well, that is what Kit and his friend are doing." Jane pulled her needle through the fabric. "Mrs. Heffelfinger told me that she and Cousin Frances' maid were to follow in the traveling coach and they would accompany her home to lend some respectability to the matter."

"I am not certain how that will happen. Lord and Lady Langford had originally approved of their match but I cannot see how they would condone an elopement." Pauline tried to imagine how her parents would feel if she had done something equally as foolish. "Sir Russell's parents no longer wished them to marry."

"They are going to be furious." It seemed Jane was of like mind. "How can this not cause a scandal?"

"Lady Frances gave us no inkling she wished to run off with Sir Russell." Pauline could be wrong but thought she remembered something entirely different. "On the contrary, I do recall her mentioning that she did not care for him."

"She must have had a change of heart. Perhaps she discovered she did care for him."

"I suppose if they wished to marry that would be the only way to manage. They cannot do it the conventional method."

"There must be some part of this we do not yet know." Jane pushed in the tip of her needle, aligning it with the previous stitches.

"How can you sit there calmly while this is going on, Jane?"

Jane looked up from her work. "There is nothing either one of us can do, Pauline. I can best help by doing as I am asked. Kit has placed me under your mother's care and I, for one, do not wish to cause any trouble."

Pauline supposed Jane must have the right of it. But still... she could not help but think there was more to Lady Frances' escapade than what they had been told. It seemed as if their families were sparing the young ladies' *delicate sensibilities* because of their age. Their families frequently considered her and Jane *too* young. Well...they would not be this age forever. Someday the two would have to be regarded as adults and not children. She and Jane were no longer girls fresh from the schoolroom.

"I cannot think she has had such a drastic change of mind as to marry Sir Russell." Pauline then had the oddest notion. Perhaps their friend had not changed her mind about the young man. Perhaps she was not a willing participant in the dash to the border. "I hope nothing untoward has happened to her."

"What are you saying, Pauline? Do you think Frances has not gone willingly? Sir Russell has *taken* her?" Apparently, the thought had not occurred to Jane, and it terrified her. "Oh no. Do not say so, Pauline."

"I am not saying that's what has happened. It's only just... well...don't you think she would have mentioned that she had reconsidered her feelings for Sir Russell to us?"

"Do you think.... Do you really...." By Jane's expression, it seemed plausible to her. "Our poor, poor Frances. She must be frightened out of her wits."

"I do hope they find her." It seemed to Pauline that this scenario they'd stumbled upon made more sense than the one they were led to believe.

"So do I," Jane whispered.

"Girls!" Mrs. Chandler called from the depths of the house, she sounded panicked. Her voice gradually grew louder until she found the two in the sitting room. "Girls!"

"What is it, Mama?" Pauline and Jane scrambled to their feet.

"Has there been any word from Sir Christopher yet?" Mrs. Chandler was quite beside herself.

"It has only been five hours, perhaps six since they have left," Jane replied. "I am certain he will send some word to us *when* he has time and when there is news."

Pauline thought *she* was the impatient one.

"And what of your brother, Pauline?" The woman motioned above her head. "He's been too long shut up in his rooms. Why can he not *do* something."

"Martin is not home, Mama," Pauline informed her. She and Jane attempted to resume their sewing.

"What's that you say?" Mrs. Chandler's demeanor changed from distressed bystander to misinformed keeper, unaware of one of her charges. "I distinctly heard him return to the house some hours ago."

"He has gone out again." Pauline bent her head, focusing on her work. "He did not say where he was going or when he would be returning." She mumbled to Jane, "I am only the *little* sister."

"He's left the house again? Where has he gone?"

"I believe he is driving in the Park."

"With a young lady?" Mrs. Chandler's voice sweetened and a smile curved her lips.

"I expect so." Pauline glanced at Jane. Even they knew that is what happened in the Park around this time. *The Fashionable Hour.*

"How very nice. Yes." Hope shone in Mrs. Chandler's eyes. "That sounds very promising indeed." She began to hum and wandered out of the room.

MARTIN WAITED AT KENNINGTON HOUSE FOR LADY EMMELINE to take their drive in Hyde Park. He had been placed in the front parlor to wait. With the various flower arrangements, it seemed to him there was barely enough room for him to stand. The staff, after sensing his discomfort, moved him to the music room.

The music room was more to his taste, there were fewer flowers, and the expanse of the room, where he could freely pace, suited him far better. He consulted his pocket watch again. If they did not leave within the next fifteen minutes they would enter the Park just as the last coach pulled out and the Fashionable Hour came to an end.

Then he began to doubt if he was supposed to take Lady Emmeline for a drive. Perhaps he had misunderstood Kit's missive and she was preparing for the ball this evening and he,

Martin, was the fool waiting belowstairs for an event that would not begin for five hours.

This was absolutely maddening. Martin returned his pocket watch to its place and pulled Kit's letter from his jacket and read it again.

I have also promised to take her for a drive in the Park at the fashionable hour this afternoon. My final commitment was to escort her to a ball given by Lady Charlotte Dolan this evening.

Martin had not been mistaken, they were to drive in the Park. He folded the letter, returned it to its pocket, then proceeded to check the time once again.

eighteen

CHRISTOPHER WAS GLAD OF his friend's company at the beginning of this journey. Albee proved a steadfast companion and seemed to share the single-minded dedication to Lady Frances' rescue. They spoke infrequently during their journey, usually when they stopped for fresh horses. As the day wore on, Christopher saw a change in his friend. There was something there now he had not seen when they left Town...a hardness and some type of disgruntled determination.

At their last stop, Albee had gone into a rant. "It is the injustice of it, Kit." He strode about. "That despot Crawford deserves everything coming to him." His boots struck the hard dirt with far more force than needed to propel him forward. A fury was building inside him.

"We will find them," Christopher vowed but could see the burning behind his friend's eyes. The darkness around them was drawing closer, which meant that the day's travel would end and the couple would stop for the night. A confrontation was inevitable.

He and Albee had ridden for many hours, currently stopping

at The Angel. Dismounting, Christopher ordered fresh horses while they stretched their legs and saw to their personal comforts. Albee took his customary stroll around the stable area looking for the yellow phaeton while Christopher talked to the ostler.

"Kit!" Albee shouted. Christopher went running and found Albee standing among the dark-colored post chaises, ornate barouches, and heavy traveling coaches. There was the yellow phaeton. The phaeton with crimson wheels could not have been common and it matched the description they'd been given from Lord Emerson's groom.

"Where is the owner of this rig?" Christopher called to the ostler who was late to follow. "What is his name?"

"*Dun* know his name, sir," the ostler replied. "You'd best check inside. I know tha' him and the Mrs have a room and stayin' for the night. I'm *ta* get his rig ready *ta* go early in the mornin'."

At the *Mrs* reference, he and Albee exchanged meaningful looks before he ran for the inn, leaving Christopher behind. He followed, arriving in time to hear his friend demand to know about the owner of the yellow phaeton and the whereabouts of the couple.

"If I am not told, I will pound on every door in this establishment until I find them," Albee threatened the proprietor. After receiving his answer, Christopher watched his friend push past everyone in his way and launch himself up the steep, narrow staircase. Albee was singularly focused and in his current state, he was not someone to be crossed.

FRANCES SAT ON A SMALL HARD CHAIR NEAR THE MODEST FIRE, ON the far side from the door. She tried to keep from shaking. Russell mistakenly believed she was cold. He had placed her where she sat now in hopes of warming her. He might have thought it was a thoughtful, caring thing to do but it could not have been further from what she desired.

The coaching inn room was adequately furnished with a bed, a small dresser, a smaller table, and two mismatched chairs. It wasn't the surroundings that bothered Frances. She wanted to know how she would escape.

She had spent the day saying everything she could think of to convince Russell this was not what they should be doing. This was not how two people got married—not two people who were supposedly in love. She suspected that tomorrow, if she should try again, would be just as useless as it had been today.

What more could Frances do? How was she to free herself? Tears welled in her eyes and she didn't want to cry, not in front of him. She didn't know how he might react or what he might do. He didn't seem to be behaving in a rational manner.

Frances wasn't cold. She wasn't hungry. She wasn't afraid. It was much worse than that, she was entirely without hope. What was to become of her?

"Dearest," Russell ran his hands down either side of her arms in what Frances believed was some attempt to comfort her. "Are you all right? Are you still cold? Shall I fetch you a wrap?"

Frances shook her head, unable to speak.

"If you prefer...." His voice softened and he drew her close. "I could warm you."

"No...." She felt his hands tighten around her arms. Now fear began to work its way through her. His breath brushed against her face and she found the scent of his day's perspiration repellent. "We are not yet wed."

"It will not be much longer...a few days more," he replied. "What will it matter?"

"Russell, I would like to go home." Despite her best effort not to become a watering pot, she thought she might at any moment break into tears. Frances turned her face away from him.

"Not just yet, *Fan*. We will return after we are married." He leaned away from the table, taking her with him. He slowly moved them from one side of the room to the other, toward the bed.

The door to the room burst open. Frances and Russell startled, separating. He had released her. Their attention fixed on the silhouetted man standing in the doorframe. The light from the fireplace and the tallow candle sitting on the table did not illuminate him well.

"What the deuce!" Russell shouted, stepping toward the intruder ready to defend.

"Lady Frances, are you unharmed?" The voice was familiar but she could not readily identify the speaker.

"I— I— am not hurt," she replied. Frances felt a glimmer of hope that this man might have come to her aid.

"You, Sir Russell Crawford will move away from Lady Frances," he demanded.

"Go to the devil!" Russell grabbed hold of the fire poker leaning against the stone surround of the hearth. He swung the poker at the man's head, who deftly ducked out of the way. "Who *are* you?"

Frances stepped back toward the table, away from the two men. She cried out when the stranger evaded a second swing of the poker when it *wooshed* by his head.

With his arms close to his sides, the man punched low, catching Russell's torso. Another few blows loosened Russell's grip on the weapon, sending it clattering to the floor.

With the next blow, the man shouted, "I am—" Russell fell backward, splaying onto his back against the dresser.

"Albert—" He moved toward his opponent. Pulling back his arm, his elbow and forearm raised high he concluded with, "Winslow."

Albert Winslow smashed Russell's face with strike after strike, the first few with his right fist then when Russell ceased to move he alternated his blows striking Russell again and again.

He must have been experiencing some type of blood-lust for he did not stop. Clearly, Russell was hardly in any condition to retaliate.

"Stop!" Frances screamed. "Stop!" Still, the punishment continued. "Please, please stop! Mr. Winslow!" she cried out. Frances felt powerless, unable to intercede.

"Albee!" Sir Christopher Glory came through the open door and ran to his friend. "AL-BEE! That is enough!" Approaching him from behind, Sir Christopher took hold of Mr. Winslow's arms and pulled him back, away from Russell.

Russell slumped against the small dresser and finally slid to the floor motionless. Frances could not quite see him clearly and concluded he must have been badly hurt.

Mr. Winslow was breathing hard and when he turned from Russell to gaze at Frances. She could see the splatter of blood.... Russell's blood...on his face and clothing.

"Have a sit, Albee." Sir Christopher navigated him toward the vacant chair near the hearth and rested his discolored hands on the table surface. Mr. Winslow said nothing and appeared to be in some sort of daze.

"Lady Frances, are you all right?" Sir Christopher glanced at Frances, his first acknowledgment of her presence.

Shaken and grateful she had not one but two liberators, she nodded.

Sir Christopher approached slowly, drew her into his arms, and held her tight. "Do not worry. You're safe now."

His warm embrace comforted her. She closed her eyes and settled against him allowing herself a few moments of relief and tears streaked down her cheeks. It was over. Frances knew that now she would be fine.

Sir Christopher settled her into a chair at the table. "We need help and I must leave you for a few moments to make arrangements." He glanced into the shadows where Russell lay. "Can you manage on your own?"

Frances nodded again and dried her eyes. Russell wasn't in any condition to cause trouble.

She was unable to pull her gaze from the man sitting at the table next to her. Mr. Winslow did not blink, he looked as if he were barely breathing. With the absence of Sir Christopher, the room was oddly silent except for the odd creaking of the floorboards and constant crackling of the fire. Not too much time passed before two women entered the room, each holding a bowl, a cloth, and a lit candle.

"Betty, over there," the first said, indicating Frances and Mr. Winslow.

"Have a look at that mort, Sally," Betty instructed.

Sally neared Russell, illuminating the corner where he lay, and moaned when she got close enough to properly see him.

Betty set the bowl she carried on the table before Frances. "Do you wish me to tend to him, m'lady?" She offered the cloth she held.

"I can manage, thank you." Frances took hold of the folded material, which she deemed clean enough, and dipped it into the water.

Betty approached the other maid near Russell. "Oooh...he's been planted a facer or two, ain't he?"

"I *spose* he's the flash cove *'oo* drew his cork?" Sally nodded in Mr. Winslow's direction.

While the women fussed around Russell, discussing what should be done next, Frances dampened the cloth and wrung out the water. There was nothing she could do about the splattered blood on his clothing and attended to his face first. He did not appear to be hurt except for the darkness across his knuckles.

"Look at your hands," she whispered, framing his bloodied appendages, contrasting with her smaller, paler trembling ones.

Frances pressed the damp cloth carefully to his knuckles, watching his face to see if she caused him any pain. He didn't move. He did not react.

Across the room, Sally and Betty had come to a consensus.

"Let's call up the lads and have this poor fella on the bed," said one of them. " 'Ee's paid for the room, *'ee* might as well use it."

CHRISTOPHER HAD BEEN GONE FOR SOME TIME. RETURNING TO Lady Frances and Albee, he opened the door slowly and stepped into the room.

Lady Frances faced in his direction when he entered. "Sir Christopher, is it time to leave yet?"

"Yes, my lady. I have brought—" He stepped to one side and allowed the woman behind him to walk past.

"Saunders!" Lady Frances launched out of her chair and dashed into the arms of her maid. Tears, he presumed of relief, streaked down her cheeks.

"*Frances!* My dear, dear girl. Thank goodness you're safe!" Mrs. Saunders hugged her charge and weeped freely. "I am so very happy to see you well. Your parents are beside themselves with worry."

"Ladies—" Christopher approached them. He noticed Albee had not moved, remaining seated in the same chair at the same spot at the table. He had been cleaned up and his hands had been bandaged. "The coach waits."

Mrs. Saunders sniffed and pulled away from the embrace and drew a shawl she'd brought across Frances' shoulders. "Come now, it is time for us to leave."

Lady Frances' lithe fingers grasped at the edges of the wrap, pulling it tight around her. She looked across the room at Russell then back at Albee. "What of Mr. Winslow?"

"I will bring him along. Do not concern yourself." Christopher reassured her.

Lady Frances nodded and allowed herself to be led to the door by her maid. Christopher watched her turn back into the dimly lit room toward the bed where Sir Russell lay. "Sir Christopher? Could you arrange to have someone sit with him?" My, she was kind-hearted. Even with his misdeeds, she could not see him neglected.

"Yes, I will see to it before we leave."

"And you'll see that he's properly cared for?"

"I will write to his father tonight."

With that Mrs. Saunders drew Frances away, down the darkened corridor to the traveling coach that waited for them.

nineteen

THEY ARRIVED AT LADY Charlotte's ball despite not caring for the other's company. It seemed they shared similar sentiments. Martin Chandler and Lady Emmeline silently made the best out of their unpleasant situation. They both tolerated the other because of their mothers' longstanding friendship and that was all.

When Martin entered the ballroom with Lady Emmeline on his arm that night, he was quite certain they shared the singular notion of only wishing to walk away from one another. They would, of course, meet again, for their agreed upon dance set. If he were asked to surrender that *opportunity* he would gladly do so without regret.

His attendance this evening was not to make the acquaintance of young ladies, nor to dance, nor to socialize. His only purpose was to escort Lady Emmeline. She might have expected more from Kit had he been present but *he* was not Kit.

Martin could hardly wait until the end of this ordeal. There were still hours to endure...first, this ball and all the guests in attendance, and second, Lady Emmeline's company.

Lady Emmeline, with Mrs. Peckover not far behind, went to her right, where a great many young ladies congregated. Martin moved purposefully to his left, where other males gathered.

"Good God, Chandler, is that you?" George Morris stepped forward. "It's been near a fortnight since I've seen you...not since...not since...."

"Bad form, Morris," Lord Harrison said with an exaggerated nudge. "Did you see who he arrived with?"

"How did you manage, Chandler?" Lord Roland squinted at him. "*Lady Emmeline....*"

Martin had been left with the burden, that's what had happened. That was not how he'd explain his predicament to the others.

"I can't even manage an introduction to her," Morris lamented.

"Perhaps we may prevail upon you...." Roland spied the rascals around him then amended, "I shall speak for myself. I'm certain she would find me agreeable...being a son of a duke and all."

"*Younger* son." Morris chortled, knowing Roland's chances of being accepted would be slim.

Martin could not say if that mattered to Lady Emmeline. He would not dare *presume*. Now, these rapscallions pressed him for an introduction. More etiquette constraints followed, making him dearly wish that he could flee.

Nothing could be worse than returning to Society when one only desired solitude. He'd noticed the odd looks and pointed stares he'd received earlier at the Venetian Breakfast that morning. Nothing was said, of course, but he had known. He *felt* it.

Now he wallowed in the midst of *this*. Martin scanned around him...the people, the unwanted attention, the unasked questions...it seemed that an introduction to Lady Emmeline outweighed the Kit and Linwood duel...*that* was old news.

"W*HO* WAS THAT MAN?"

"*Mister* Chandler?" Hester Enfield uttered Emmeline's escort's name as if it were the most unpalatable mouthful of syllabub.

Em did not wish to waste a single moment thinking about him. She could not understand what was wrong with Martin Chandler. It was as if he had not even noticed her, much less complimented her on her fine appearance. Her toilette was not completed with him in mind nor was her choice of gown. It was always her desire to appear at her best, at every occasion.

They had barely uttered a word to one another during the entire drive to Lady Charlotte's ball, only to arrange for a country dance later that night. Em imagined that was only because it was expected of him. It was of no matter, she would have plenty of gentlemen to fill her dance card.

But really...the man was intolerable.

Her small group of friends noticed the efforts of her splendid toilette and admired her peach-edged gown. Em smiled, relishing their kind words regarding her appearance.

"I thought Sir Christopher was to escort you tonight," Lady Amelia boldly inquired.

"Was he not your escort at the Venetian Breakfast this morning?" Miss Danvers, whom Em had not seen at the Breakfast, asked.

"I believe he was but...." Miss Carter replied to Lady Amelia then turned to Emmeline. "But did you not take a drive in the Park with Mr. Chandler this afternoon?"

"Mr. Chandler was kind enough to assume Sir Christopher's obligations," Em informed the ladies. "Apparently, he has been unexpectedly called away regarding a pressing family matter."

"Did you really expect Sir Christopher to escort you to all these activities all day today?" Miss Carter must not have seen the unique opportunity of having Sir Christopher all to oneself.

"Of course, whyever not?" Em would have been delighted to have shared his company.

"It is quite a lot of time to spend with one person, is it not?" Miss Carter appeared concerned.

"Not in Sir Christopher's case." Em smiled, thinking just how different, how splendid the Breakfast and the drive in the Park would have been in the baronet's company.

"One must commend Mr. Chandler for coming to the aid of his friend," Lady Amelia replied, who could not have preferred him over Sir Christopher.

"Yes, I suppose Mr. Chandler was kind to do so." Em kept her personal opinions to herself, spending the day with him was unfortunate.

"I cannot imagine you would consider Mr. Chandler a possible suitor." Miss Danvers, who had knowledge of Em's thoughts on that matter commented.

"No," Em stated quite emphatically. "I do not."

THE RESCUE OF LADY FRANCES HAD BEEN A SUCCESS. THEIR GROUP had spent the night at a respectable country inn before they embarked on the return to Town.

As far as Albert understood, Kit had made many hasty preparations for them concerning the rescue of Lady Frances upon their departure the previous day. He had kept several family members informed as to their progress and notified inns along the Great North Road of their arrival. Conversely, for her recovery, Kit had taken some time and gone to great pains to make Lady Frances' return to Town as easy and comfortable as he could.

"We are to meet the ladies in the private parlor in a half hour for breakfast." Kit stood before the cheval glass wrestling with the collar, shirt points, and his neckcloth. He and Albert shared this room in this fairly shabby establishment, having reserved the inn's finest for the ladies. "Some people may prefer not to partake in an early morning meal but I know that ain't you."

"Nor is it you," Albert returned. His friend could have easily devoured two entire chickens and a joint of ham by himself given enough time.

"Will you be able to ride?" Kit finished tying his cravat and glanced at Albert who had lost use of his digits. He did not even make use of a mirror. "Because you certainly cannot dress yourself."

"I will manage." He held the neckerchief with the tips of his index and middle fingers, unable to tie the simple knot it required.

"Certainly not with that scarf, but perhaps you'll do better with the reins. All right, now stand still."

Albert straightened, tipped his chin upward, and remained still while Kit played valet.

"You could ride in the coach," Kit suggested, refolding the piece before placing it around Albert's neck. Kit pulled the two ends of the cloth forward, crossed them, and tied a neat square knot.

"With the ladies?" Albert did not think that a good idea. It would be too close to *her* for too long, making the journey agony for him.

"I do not believe they would think you unmanly for doing so. Here, you go." Kit picked up Albert's jacket for him to don.

"No, I'm not worried about appearing *unmanly*." He pushed his arm through one sleeve then shifted to carefully work his other arm through the second. Albert glanced at himself in the glass. He could barely face his own reflection and could not bear to look himself in the eyes.

He felt ashamed for what he'd done, how he behaved before Lady Frances last night. True, she had been successfully rescued but his actions were reprehensible, and it bothered him greatly.

"There, what do you think?" Kit stood back and allowed Albert to admire his reflection in the glass.

"I'm sure my horse will consider himself lucky to have such a dapper rider upon his back. Thank you." He touched the knot at his throat and assured himself that the ends would not work themselves loose.

"Didn't do it for you or the horse, did it for the ladies who'll have to share a breakfast table with you." Kit clapped him on the back. "All right, let's go before they've eaten all the rashers."

"After you." Albert did not have much of an appetite this morning, even though he had ridden for a great majority of the day yesterday and eaten nothing.

He was not particularly feeling proud of himself and considered himself lucky if Lady Frances didn't completely despise him. There was no use killing a man or even beating him senseless after one had gained the upper hand. He and Kit had saved the damsel in distress and that should have been the end of it.

"HAVE YOU LADIES HAD ENOUGH TO EAT?" SIR CHRISTOPHER sipped on his third cup of coffee following his very hearty breakfast and checked with all the females of his party. Frances imagined he had eaten double the amount of all three women combined.

"What would your mother say if she saw you making a glutton of yourself?" Mrs. Hefflefinger, who had a modest spoonful of eggs and two pieces of toast, must have felt it was out of character for him.

"After she realized that I had not eaten all day yesterday, Lady Yardley would say, 'Would you care for fifths, Christopher?'" in a voice meant to mimic his mother. The ladies chuckled, amused with the imitation.

Mr. Winslow did not smile, finding very little humor, and ate nearly nothing.

"If you will excuse me, ladies and Mr. Winslow, I think I will check on our travel preparations." Sir Christopher lowered his cup and saucer and rose from the table. "Mrs. Heffelfinger, a word, if you please?" He moved toward the door and motioned that she should follow, which Mrs. Heffelfinger did at once.

"Shall I leave you in the company of Mr. Winslow? You should be safe enough in this private parlor. I wish to check that our trunks are packed and our wraps and bonnets are waiting." Saunders pushed away from the table.

"We shall be fine." Frances smiled, believing there was probably no one with whom she would be safer. "Perhaps I will have another cup of chocolate in a bit."

"Is there something I can fetch for you now that I am up, Mr. Winslow?"

"No, thank you, Mrs. Saunders." The man barely shifted in his chair. It was the most he'd moved since the group had sat for their meal.

The lady's maid left the room, closing the door behind her, leaving Mr. Winslow alone with Frances.

"How are you feeling this morning, Mr. Winslow? Are you well?" Frances could imagine he might be poorly. He had pushed his food around the plate and not once during the meal had he glanced in her direction. "I must admit I am somewhat concerned about you."

"I feel I must apologize for my actions last night," Mr. Winslow said. "It may appear that I had overreacted. I confess that I cannot abide to see a lady in need of aid...."

"You have nothing to apologize for, sir. I am most grateful to you and Sir Christopher." Frances swallowed hard, she felt herself growing quite emotional. "I truly felt quite despondent before your arrival. I did not think anyone would follow, much less find us."

"There were many who were at wit's end." He pushed his plate aside and leaned back in his chair.

"Goodness—what of my parents!" So concerned was she for her own well-being, Frances had not given a thought to her family and what they must be thinking.

"Kit—Sir Christopher has written to Lord Langford assuring him of your safe return on the morrow. You needn't worry."

Thank goodness someone had the mind to notify her family of her rescue.

"Tomorrow?" Frances, somewhat confused, did not wish to bother with the maths but did it not take a day's travel to get this far?

"We will not be traveling near the speed of the phaeton, nor will we be on the road for the same number of hours," he told her. "You shall be home in time for tea and to attend Almack's if that is your wish."

"That is good to know." Frances chuckled. "And I do not have an invitation to Almack's." She noticed a hint of a smile touching his lips at her retort. It lightened her heart to know he was able to find a way through the gray clouds he appeared to be under just a few moments ago.

"Be that as it may, if you had, you would arrive in plenty of time." After freely gesturing with his hand, he must have forgotten it was injured, he lowered it, making certain to keep both appendages below the surface of the table and out of her line of sight. "Sir Christopher has also written to Lord Emerson informing him of his son's actions, present condition, and where he is to be found." Mr. Winslow grew quiet once more then whispered, "I expect the earl will send someone to fetch him if he does not do so himself. In any case, I do not expect Sir Russell will be spending his recovery in Town."

"No, I don't expect so." Their attempted dash to Gretna must have raised an uproar and caused a scandal for certain. Removing Russell to their country estate might be the best place for their family to spend the remainder of the year. "I'm afraid Sir Russell was confused. I believe he thought he loved me. That's why he did it...out of desperation."

"I do not believe one displays their affection with hidden agendas and deception." Mr. Winslow gazed at her from across the table.

"Yes, of course, you're right." Frances could not argue that. There was something in the way he gazed at her, a steadiness... an *admiration*? For her? He was the one who had saved her. It was something, she admitted, she could not have done herself. "I cannot tell you how grateful I am to you."

They shared a quiet moment. Both understood the danger and what might have happened if Mr. Winslow had not arrived when he had.

"You should not have been subject to that brutal attack on your abductor," he said. "Again, I must sincerely apologize." How could he feel so remorseful when he had saved her?

"I thought your *punishment* harsh at first but now I realize if you had not incapacitated him, he might have done the same to you...or worse."

"I could not bear his—" The muscles in Mr. Winslow's jaw twitched and he closed his eyes. Frances could see the battle inside of him as he worked to suppress his anger. "*That man* was not to be tolerated. I do not know how else we would have stopped him and I'm quite certain you could not have done so on your own."

"The outcome might have been so much worse for me. Never fear, Mr. Winslow. I will not allow that one day, no matter how atrocious, to taint the remaining days of my life." She turned from him to gaze out the small window that faced the front of the establishment for just a moment. "Do you know there was a point where I nearly gave up hope? Then you came through the door."

He lowered his head, bringing his gloved hand to his face. Was it in regret? It was as if he did not want to be reminded of the moment.

"I am indebted to you." Frances could not hide the tears in her eyes when she reached across to him and placed her hand upon his arm. "You have returned the rest of my life to me, Mr. Winslow. Do not allow the very same brave action to deprive you of yours."

Taking in her words, Albert looked from Lady Frances' hand resting upon his arm and gazed into her face...into her eyes and smiled.

End of Book One

**Grace, Lady Yardley
Marriages**

1 Squire John Swithins

Henry Swithins

2 Anthony Pomeroy

Samuel Pomeroy

William Pomeroy

3 Sir George Glory

Sir Christopher Glory

4 Right Hon John Abbott

Victoria Abbott

John Abbott
(heir presumptive
Earl of Langford)

**5 Robert Stiles
Viscount Wyman**

The Hon Jane Stiles

Robert Stiles
Viscount Wyman

6 The Hon Samuel Everett

Simon Everett

Edward Everett

**7 Edward Clifton
Earl of Barlow**

William Clifton
Earl of Barlow

The Hon Frederick
Clifton

**8 The Lord Robert
Beeson**

Stephen Beeson

Peter Beeson

**9 Andrew Tuttle
Marquis of Worsham**

Anthony Tuttle
Marquis of Worsham

The Lord James Tuttle

**10 The Lord Yardley
Grayson**

Hilary Grayson

Richard Grayson

Abbott Family Tree
(Earl of Langford)

Arthur, Earl of Langford	Margaret, Countess of Langford

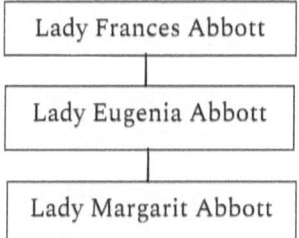

Lady Frances Abbott

Lady Eugenia Abbott

Lady Margarit Abbott

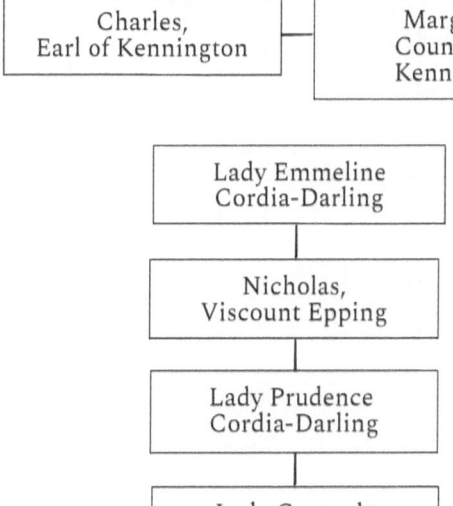

Cordia-Darling Family Tree (Earl of Kennington)

Charles, Earl of Kennington — Margaret, Countess of Kennington

Lady Emmeline Cordia-Darling

Nicholas, Viscount Epping

Lady Prudence Cordia-Darling

Lady Gertrude Cordia-Darling

about the author

California-born Shirley Marks lives in Silicon Valley with her software engineer husband and unpredictable Australian Cattle Dog mix. Shirley dreams of returning to London, Paris, and Florence to research settings, develop new characters, and stories to weave together for her upcoming novel. When at home, she spends time reading, writing, and trying to get the odd knitting project completed.

Shirley writes Traditional Regency Romance stories (sweet/clean), clean Romantic Comedies, and a couple of paranormal novels.

You can visit Shirley at: www.ShirleyMarks.com